Star Crossed

MADDIE JAMES

SAND DUNE BOOKS

Star Crossed

Maddie James

A Falls Mountain Romance
Book 4

About Falls Mountains

Welcome to Harbor Falls—where second chances bloom, hearts heal, and love finds its way home in the Blue Ridge Mountains.

The *Falls Mountain Romance* series delivers heartfelt, semi-sweet love stories filled with small-town charm, found family, and the promise of new beginnings. Each book can be read as a standalone story, but together they celebrate the beauty of hope, healing, and happily ever after.

But on Falls Mountain, love has a habit of showing up unannounced.

From second chances to secret babies to grumpy-sunshine pairings, each book brings a satisfying happily-ever-after and a cast of characters you'll want to visit again and again.

Falls Mountain Romance is a companion series to the Sweet Hart Inn Romance books by Maddie James.

Star Crossed

A first love worth fighting for. A truth fifteen years overdue. A second chance that could change everything.

When children's advocate attorney Jasmine Walker returns to Harbor Falls after fifteen years away, she expects to settle her foster mother's estate and slip quietly back to Atlanta. Instead, she collides with Jack Ackerman—the only boy she ever loved, and the man she left without a word.

Jack never understood why Jasmine ran. One look at her now and all the years in between fall away. When Ms. Leinie's final wishes tie Jasmine to a new community project—and to Jack—neither can avoid the past they've tried so hard to outrun.

But Harbor Falls holds more than memories. It holds secrets. Pain. And the echo of a love that once burned bright under the Carolina stars.

As revelations unfold and emotions rekindle, Jasmine must decide if she can finally stop running... And Jack must decide whether to take a second chance on the only woman he's ever loved.

A heartfelt, emotional small-town romance about forgiveness, hope, and finding your way back home.

Why you'll love this book:

- Emotional second-chance romance
- Heart-filled small-town setting
- Protective hero who never stopped loving her
- Foster-care themes with depth
- Feels like curling up with a blanket on a cool mountain night

Obituary—Mrs. Madeleine Harbor Crockett

THE HARBOR FALLS LEADER

HARBOR FALLS, NC: Mrs. Madeleine Harbor Crockett, 83, known to the Harbor Falls community as Ms. Leinie, passed away on July 4 in the comfort of her home after a year-long illness. A lifelong resident of Harbor Falls, she was preceded in death by an infant son, Christopher, and her husband Christoph Crockett, a former instructor at Harbor Falls Community College, and an adjunct professor at several North Carolina regional universities over the years.

Ms. Leinie's family was among the founders of the community of Harbor Falls; her great-grandfather considered an instrumental leader in the early community. Thus, the town name. Her father served as the mayor of Harbor Falls for a decade. Ms. Leinie was a member of the Harbor Falls United Methodist Church, where a public celebration of her life will be held on Sunday at two o'clock in the afternoon. In life, Ms. Leinie was a private woman who enjoyed children and her rescue pets. Over the years, she gave shelter to many of both—

children and pets—when they most needed love, care, and affection.

Ms. Leinie is survived by a distant cousin, Margaret Harbor Drake, of Oregon. Instead of flowers, Ms. Leinie requests donations sent to the Harbor Falls Animal Shelter or to the Harbor Falls Children's Foundation.

Chapter One

They say you can never go home again.

Jasmine Walker stepped out of her Audi and browsed the streets of her old hometown. Determined to focus on the positive aspects of the day, all she wanted was to take care of business, and get out of Harbor Falls and back to Atlanta before nightfall.

She sniffed at the crisp mountain air drifting into the valley town from the Blue Ridge Mountains, a hint of spruce and lingering wood smoke tickling her nostrils. The nights and mornings were cool now, and even though it was approaching ten o'clock in the morning, the temperature was chilly. She pulled her jacket together and buttoned it.

The breeze played with her hair for a moment. Closing her eyes, she paused to let the essence of the town settle around her. She blinked, then moved out of the way and closed the car door. She headed for the sidewalk, turned, and scanned the town once more, glancing right and left.

Settling her gaze in the opposite direction from her destination, she searched just above the treetops, traveling the length of the street. Victorian shop fronts graced both sides, with mature trees, potted plants, streetlights, and awnings, complete with small-town hustle and bustle.

Some things had changed. There were a few new stores, ones that if she'd had more time, she wouldn't mind browsing —something she never did when she'd lived there. She spotted a local gift shop across the street next to a bakery, and it looked like the library might have undergone an expansion. She'd spent a lot of time there as a kid. Much of the town was the same, however, as when she'd left fifteen years earlier.

What she was looking for wasn't on the sidewalk or at the street level though, but in the distance above the buildings and trees.

There.

Ms. Leinie's house.

Her stomach clutched as her gaze drifted up behind the courthouse to the big, white house on the hill a few blocks away—the one she had once called home. Suddenly, she had to shake herself. She'd been sad to learn of Ms. Leinie's death, and had it not been for the call from Art Manchester, a local attorney, Jasmine might not have known. On the other hand, she might have belatedly found out and sent a donation and simply reflected on her relationship with the old woman back in the safe confines of her condominium.

Reflecting on the positives, of course, and not the negatives.

She strove to live an optimistic life. Glass half full, and all that. It hadn't always been that way.

But the call came, and she'd made the day trip back to Harbor Falls.

An older model pickup truck with country music blaring whizzed by, pulling her out of her musing, and reminding her of the more-than-subtle differences between Harbor Falls and Atlanta.

Jasmine glanced at her watch. She had ten minutes until her appointment with the attorney. Turning, she headed back up Main Street but stopped long enough to push a few coins into her parking meter before moving on. Two hours should be enough. She didn't expect to be long here in Harbor Falls. There was nothing to keep her, no one to see while she was in town. She'd severed all of those ties years ago. Two hours should be ample time to deal with the business of Ms. Leinie's estate and then head back home. She had a case that needed her attention tonight.

Her heels clicked on the sidewalk as she made her way down the street, a nagging question lingering in her head.

Why, after all this time, had Leinie Crockett left anything to her?

"So, you broke up with her?"

Jack Ackerman winced at his brother's question. Instead of immediately responding, he stared ahead through the windshield and concentrated on driving down the two-lane road on Harbor Falls Mountain. He really wasn't up to talking much about the recent events with Miss Nora Patterson.

"Jack?"

"I figured you knew."

"No. Not until this morning when Mom called."

Hell. He braked for a curve and nearly threw his brother into the door. "Mom called?"

"She heard it down at Ralph's."

"Shit." He twisted the radio button to crank up Blake Shelton, hoping to drown out the noise clattering in his head. That's all he needed, for every woman of marrying age in Harbor Falls to be on his tail. How many single, thirty-four-year-old men were there out there, anyway? Not many.

And he didn't need the grocery store gossipmongers on the trail.

They traveled along for several minutes, turning at the foot of the mountain to head along Lake Road, and then into downtown Harbor Falls. They each needed to run a couple of errands and then get back out to Haven's Hill to prep for a big landscaping job at Suzie Hart's Sweet Hart Inn later in the week. Seemed she was hosting some fancy to-do with some New York bigwigs, and all that. He wouldn't let his friend down.

Finally, he glanced at Sam. "Yeah. We broke up."

Sam shrugged. "I don't get it."

"It's for the best."

"Becca never said a word."

That surprised him. Becca and Nora being best friends and all, and Becca being Sam's wife. "Guess that kills our euchre game night."

He saw Sam's nod out of the corner of his eye. Jack slowed as he approached Main Street and searched for a street parking space.

"Over there by the bank." Sam nodded that way.

"Want me to drop you off at the hardware store?"

"Naw, I'll walk."

Jack parallel parked the pickup and turned to Sam. "Guess I'll have to ditch out of that couples thing up at the lodge on Saturday too. Hope you and Becca understand. Not sure I'm up for it."

Sam's brows furled. "That woman do a number on you?"

He shook his head. "Nope. It was mutual, actually. The relationship wasn't going anywhere, and honestly, I wasn't in love with her. Not like you are in love with Becca." *I want more. Like kids. The picket fence. Normal.*

"There will be a lot of women up there at the lodge on Saturday." Sam waggled his brows.

"It's a couples thing, remember?"

"Sure, but it's a benefit for the hospital, so I don't think they'll kick you out on your ear because you don't have a date."

Jack winced. "Yeah, but count me out. Not in the mood."

"Ah, that's alright." Sam opened the truck door. "I'll meet you back here in about twenty minutes. Just need a pair of long screws."

Jack chuckled and watched his brother head down the sidewalk. *You and me both, buddy.*

JASMINE, 1999

Breathless, I pushed into the kitchen, letting the back screen door slap a mite too hard behind me. "Oops! So sorry, Ms. Leinie." I'd practically sprinted the entire way home from school, nearly giddy at what I knew the future held for me.

"Jasmine! Honey, what's the hurry?"

Ms. Leinie turned away from the stove and smiled. In so many ways, I hated thinking about leaving, because Ms. Leinie had really been the only woman to ever influence my life—but graduation was just three weeks away.

It's inevitable. I'm aging out of foster care and I have to think of my future.

Stepping to the refrigerator, I said, "I know you are cooking, but I'm starved. Mind if I have an apple? You know I have an appetite from hell, and it won't spoil my supper." I reached for the handle.

"Lord knows you have a bottomless pit for a stomach, girl. Go ahead. And don't say 'hell'."

"Sorry." Ms. Leinie liked all of us kids to keep our mouths clean. "It's from running track. I burn it all off."

5

"You been running this afternoon? You're all hot and sweaty." She stirred the pot and side-glanced at me.

Removing an apple from the fruit bin, I stepped to the sink to wash it off, then moved closer to the stove and glanced into the pot. "Oh, vegetable soup. Homemade. I love you, Ms. Leinie." I threw my arms around her next and kissed her cheek.

Her skin was paper thin and reminded me of tissue paper. I wasn't sure how old Ms. Leinie was, but I guessed her to be in her late sixties. She was a practical woman and dressed simply, with her hair pulled back. There were days I wondered how long it was, because most times I saw it in a clip and off her face. It was white-gray, but I could see wisps of dark curls at the nape. There were times I would sit and study her while she didn't know I was looking. I imagined in her younger years, she was a striking woman.

I often wondered what my mother would have looked like as an older woman.

"No, not running today. Just hurrying to get home, and it's heating up out there for May. But I have some exciting news! Promise me you won't tell anyone. It's like a pinky-swear thing."

Ms. Leinie looked at me and grinned. "Well now, I haven't had to pinky-swear on anything in a long time. What's up, Jasmine? I bet you got that music award."

"No. No." I grinned. "Well, maybe. They won't announce those until graduation night. I'm still in the running for it, and the cash could really help with my college expenses." I paused and watched as she nodded in agreement but couldn't contain my excitement any longer. The words bubbled out. "Jack asked me to marry him. We're getting married."

Her face fell. And something icky landed in the pit of my stomach.

She reached for my hand. "Jasmine, honey, come sit down

and let's talk about this." She tugged at my hand, but I couldn't move. Her tone, her words...none of it was good. My excitement was abruptly squashed.

After a moment, I found my feet, drifted toward the table, and sat.

She looked me in the eye and patted my hand. "You know the Ackermans will never allow this marriage. Right?"

She'd warned me before about the Ackermans. I'd met both of Jack's parents and his older brother Sam. Most of the time I just saw them from afar at the ball games and in town. They were always nice but distant. I knew why. I tried not to let it bother me.

Jack had been my boyfriend since football season. I played the flute in the band, and he, of course, was on the team. The band went to all the away games, and before I knew it, we were catching each other's gazes, and it didn't take long for us to become a couple. Jack loved me for who I am, no matter what. We were head-over-heels in love, as they say. "Well, that's why we're waiting until after graduation to really make any plans. They don't know yet, and Jack isn't going to tell them right away. We'll get married this summer and then move to Asheville and go to school. We'll get jobs and support ourselves. We'll be fine."

The look on her face puzzled me. Then she said, "Jasmine, think about this. Because you are in foster care, the state will take care of your college expenses, and all of that. But if you get married, all of that stops. How will you support yourself and pay for college at the same time? You don't want to discount all of that. Why don't you and Jack just wait?"

I'd already thought about all of that. "It's okay. I have it all worked out. I don't want to rely on the state if I don't have to. I want to be self-sufficient. Besides, there are work-study programs that I've already applied to and I'm eligible for, and I will get the Social Security income from my mom, plus I get a little money because of Dad...."

Ms. Leinie interrupted. "Jasmine, I understand all of that. It's just—"

I smiled and tried to look upbeat. "It will be fine! Really!"

But she wasn't buying it. "Honey, I fear you are setting yourself up for a whole world of hurt. I don't want your sweet little heart to get broken. I swear, sometimes you can be so gullible. The Ackermans will never accept this."

Gullible?

I felt a little prickly inside, defensive, and unsure why I felt the need to state my case. Ms. Leinie wasn't the enemy, and I knew fully well how Jack's parents felt. I stood up. "It doesn't matter. Jack and I love each other, and—"

"You don't have to leave here, Jasmine," she interrupted. "Don't get married because you think you don't have a home. You can stay here until you get on your feet. You're still so young."

"Ms. Leinie. It's not that. I love Jack."

She stood then, too, and took both of my hands in hers. She shook them gently. "Jasmine, you listen to me. I have to be honest. You've been with me for so long, and I feel like your mama in so many ways. I'm going to talk to you like a mama would. Let Jack go off to college, you too, and then later, down the road, if you feel the same about each other, think about getting married then. Live some life first. Don't tie yourself down."

I eyed her, watching the concern grow on her face. "Being young is not what you're concerned about, is it, Ms. Leinie? You know Jack's parents don't like me. You know they think I'm not good enough for Jack, considering my background. But Jack loves me. We love each other. That's all that matters, right?"

Her eyes welled up with tears. She pulled me closer and

hugged me. I remember that hug well because it was the last one she ever gave me. It was warm and firm, but laced with a strange sense of desperation and apprehension.

She pulled back. "Honey, I love your heart, but not everyone has a giving and kind heart that you do. If you marry Jack, I fear your happy heart will turn. The Ackermans won't—"

"Just say it, Ms. Leinie. Just say what's on your mind."

Her lips clamped shut. I stared at her until she finally said it.

"Okay. Jasmine, this is a small town. You know this. And even though it's almost the 21st century, it's still the conservative South. There are many people who are not so liberal. The Ackermans are like that. And well…"

She paused and took a deep breath.

I knew where this was going. I didn't breathe at all for many seconds.

"Well," she continued, "they will not stand by and let their youngest boy run off and get married to…you."

"To me."

She nodded slowly, a pained expression on her face. "To a little mixed girl."

A little mixed girl.

My heart turned right then, on the spot. I broke the grasp of Ms. Leinie's hands and slowly backed away, our gazes connected. I knew she didn't mean to sound so harsh, but in my naïve little heart, that's how I took it.

"You mean a half-breed, Black girl don't you?" Because she'd always be half-Black, but never half-white.

She took a step forward. "Jasmine."

I backed off.

"Fine," I said, right before I left the kitchen, "then I'll just take my poor half-Black trash self out of this town and, by

9

God, I will not look back. Thank you for everything, Ms. Leinie."

Then I turned and raced for the stairs, knowing I was placing the blame where it shouldn't be placed, saying things that made no sense. I heard her calling after me, but the white noise in my head wouldn't let her words in.

Chapter Two

J asmine drummed her fingers on Art Manchester's oversized, polished mahogany desktop, waiting for him to return. She glanced at the typical décor. His office was pretty much par for the course for a small-town attorney. It was a pleasant office on Main Street, a corner abode, on the second floor of the bank and trust building. Shelves with rows of leather-bound books lined the room, except for one enormous picture window overlooking the town of Harbor Falls. Everything was mahogany and leather. A nice, conservative look. Heavy wooden filing cabinets stood in the corner.

Yes, in her experience, typical. Totally the opposite of her office in Atlanta. Of course, she was not your typical lawyer. Jasmine took on both high-profile and court-appointed family and child advocate cases in the city of Atlanta. And there were plenty of both. Her office was brighter, welcoming to children and families. She had a reading corner with shelves full of children's books and a low table with crayons and paper and puzzles. There was a soft sofa for parents, so they could relax and feel more at home, while Jasmine discussed some very serious and difficult subjects with them.

Art obviously practiced small-town general law and, she thought, must do it well. Funny, she didn't remember him from when she lived in Harbor Falls—but as a child she was caught up in her own little world, and then at eighteen, of course, she left and never looked back.

She likely had little in common with this Art Manchester. He looked established and settled, with a pretty blonde wife, if the picture on his desk was any sign. And if the law books stacked on his desk were any further indication, he was currently handling a variety of issues—contracts, civil suits, wills and trusts.

Wills and trusts. That's what she was here for.

The door behind her creaked, and Art rushed back into the room. He sat, opened up a folder, and then looked up to Jasmine.

"I'm sorry for the delay, but I needed to run downstairs to the bank."

"I understand," she said.

He looked her in the eyes, and Jasmine straightened her back, waiting. "As you know from our discussion on the phone, Ms. Leinie Crockett passed away last week, and you were specifically named in her will."

Jasmine scooted to the edge of her seat. "Yes. You mentioned that. I'm curious but wonder if there is a mistake. I left Ms. Leinie's home when I was eighteen. I've not spoken with her since."

Art shook his head. "No mistake. Let me read you a small snippet of her last will and testament." He placed a pair of reading glasses on the bridge of his nose.

"To Ms. Jasmine Walker," he began, "whom I loved like a daughter..." As he began reading, a queasiness settled over her stomach. She should have eaten breakfast, but she wanted to get on the road soon to avoid the Atlanta rush hour later.

He cleared his throat, and Jasmine realized she'd become distracted. She looked back at him and watched the paper in his hand.

"...I leave just one thing. The contents of my safe deposit box at First Harbor Falls B&T. What she does with it is up to her." He looked up and waited.

"That's it?"

He nodded. "Yes. That's it."

"What's in the box?"

He shook his head then. "I don't know, but here is the key." He unclipped a small envelope from the folder and handed it to her. The envelope had #352 written on the outside.

"Now what?"

Art stood. "Now we'll head downstairs to see what's in the box. We'll meet with Carl Robbins, the bank official who will take us to the safety deposit area. He has the other key. I'll leave you at that point, since my official work will be done. You are an attorney and likely don't need my advice, but if you'd like me to stick around, just let me know."

Jasmine couldn't imagine there could be much in the box, so she figured she'd send him on his way and be done with it all quickly. Glancing at her watch, she realized she could be on her way back to Atlanta in no time. That thought gave her great relief. She was ready to get back home. Being here in Harbor Falls made her nervous.

Ms. Leinie lived simply, even though she had that big old, beautiful house, so whatever was in the box was likely small and sentimental. Perhaps some jewelry or maybe some recipes. She had always loved Ms. Leinie's cooking. Yes, that was probably it. Jasmine had always teased that she wanted her recipe box after she had passed.

A pang hit her gut, and she almost teared up.

Jasmine jerked her head up and stood. "All right. Let's go."

JACK LEFT THE TRUCK AND HEADED ACROSS THE street to the bank. As he pulled on the brass door handle, the heavy oak door swung open, hitting him with a blast of air-conditioned air. He stepped across the lobby toward the first clerk's window and, glancing about, asked if Cam Parker was available.

"He stepped out for about five minutes, Mr. Ackerman," the bank clerk said. "Why don't you have a seat, and I'll let him know as soon as he returns."

Jack needed to get the details on Ms. Leinie's construction account from Cam. Ms. Leinie had contracted him to oversee the construction of the building over on Court Street. They'd started this project before she passed, of course. Art Manchester had called him last week to tell him to continue, and that Cam Parker had the details about the account and how he would get paid, and also how he would pay for the crew and materials.

They had halted construction temporarily until everything was worked out. In a way, he was glad. Being the general contractor for the project was side work for him. He and Sam had owned Haven's Hill Nursery for the past ten years, and that was his primary job. But he enjoyed construction too. It all kept his hands busy, and that was a good thing.

Busy hands, busy mind. Lately, he needed to keep both occupied.

Breaking up with Nora hadn't been an easy thing to do. They'd been a couple for months, and he'd been contemplating the breakup for about half that time. He had never been that good at confrontation, especially when it was going to hurt someone. He feared he had hurt Nora's feelings badly. It couldn't be helped, though. He and Nora wanted different things in life, and at thirty-four, he wasn't ready to settle—he was ready to get on with what he really wanted in life. He knew he couldn't let much more dust settle under his heels.

Nodding to the clerk, he was headed across the lobby when he heard voices coming from one of the other offices. He glanced up to see Art Manchester and Carl Robbins leave the office with a tall, nicely dressed woman. They turned toward the back hallway, which led to the vault where the safety deposit boxes were located.

The three stopped to chat.

Jack started to sit but something about the woman gave him pause.

Her hair... The color of dark honey with flecks of gold. He'd only seen that color once before, and there had been times in his life when he would have given anything to see it again.

He straightened and squared his shoulders.

The woman looked straight at him.

Jasmine.

———

"THANK YOU FOR YOUR TIME, MR. ROBBINS. I'M sure this will only take a minute," Jasmine stated as she and the two men stepped into the lobby.

Carl Robbins nodded. "Of course. I'm happy to help, Ms. Walker." Then he stopped and added, "I am so sorry to learn of your loss."

My loss? Oh. She nodded. "Yes, Ms. Leinie was a friend to everyone, though, wasn't she?"

"She was indeed."

Jasmine glanced off, movement at the front of the bank

catching her eye. The sight of a man standing several feet away startled her, and she wasn't entirely sure why. Perhaps it was the way his body was squared and planted in the center of the bank facing her, and how he was looking straight at her. With familiarity....

He started walking toward them, and her gaze traveled up to his face.

No.

Turning away, she moved toward the hallway, hoping the men were following suit. Her chest, suddenly constricted and full of fluttering butterflies, ached. Her stomach took on an immediate queasiness that was difficult to ignore. She glanced at her watch and said loudly, "I have a dinner engagement at seven in Atlanta. Could we hurry this along?"

That was a lie. She didn't care.

Jack. It was him. Wasn't it?

She didn't look back. Wouldn't.

"Jasmine?"

She'd briefly contemplated on her drive up to Harbor Falls how she would react if she coincidentally ran into him today. She'd brushed away the idea as absurd. She hadn't heard from Jack in years and assumed he was married with kids by now. Of course, that would be easier, wouldn't it? If he was married with a wife and children?

Somehow, she didn't want to think of that either. Jack, wife, kids....

She dismissed it all. She was not here to think about or talk with Jack Ackerman.

"Jasmine?" The voice, male and urgent, broke through the haze in her brain. She stopped up short, realizing she had walked several feet into the hallway.

Alone.

She turned. Jack stood there, flanked on either side by Art

Manchester and Carl Robbins. His face was a puzzle. Probably much like what she felt like on the inside.

"Jack?" Her voice was barely a whisper. Then, she squared her shoulders and said with more conviction, "Jack. Wow. It's been a long time."

He stepped forward. "Too long." Several more steps and he was in front of her, his voice softer now. "Jazzy, you look..." He searched her eyes. "Incredible."

Jazzy....

The way he said his nickname for her... The way the word slipped off his tongue and fell onto her ears and into her heart... It brought a wealth of pleasant, confusing and even painful images to her mind, and to her quivering tummy....

It was as if fifteen years turned on a dime.

He was the one who looked incredible. If she let the truth get the better of her, she'd say he looked *more* than incredible. He looked, well, handsome, and sexy, and swoon-worthy, and fabulous, and... "Jack, thank you. You look well."

Well? Okay, that was safe. Yes. Keep it safe.

He looked more than well. Whatever work he was doing kept him trim and fit, all six-foot-two inches of him. His dark, close-cut hair held a hint of silver, which reflected nicely in his light blue eyes. Looking well was a misnomer. The man was positively hot.

"What are you doing in Harbor Falls?" He reached for her hand. Touched her. Then hesitantly pulled back. She did, too. Her skin burned where they'd connected.

"Oh, Ms. Leinie... She, well. There is a safe deposit box and..."

"Will you be here this evening? How about dinner?"

She shook her head. "No."

Jack's face fell, and she felt awful that she'd said that one word with a little more conviction than she had intended.

"I mean, thank you, but no, Jack. I need to get back to

Atlanta tonight. Once I finish here..." She looked to the other two men standing a few feet away, then back to him. She smiled. "It's great to see you, but I have to take care of a few things and then be on my way."

She stepped back, and an ache the size of Falls Mountain landed in the pit of her stomach. She looked at Mr. Robbins. "Should we move on?"

Jack interjected. "Jasmine, how can I...?"

The question fell into thin air as Jasmine turned and said, "Goodbye, Jack. Talk soon?" She knew there would be no talking soon, but she had just enough Southern manners to make the effort.

Her heels clicked on the hard tile floor as she headed deeper into the hallway and further away from Jack. Her brain registered the last look on his face, his gaze searching for hers, the look of a sudden sense of loss upon it. Still, she searched his eyes. For some connection, some hint of...something?

Married with children, she reminded herself. Why on earth would he not be by now? *I mean, look at him?*

Breathless, and for no apparent reason other than that seeing Jack had sucked the air out of her lungs, they rounded a corner and came up short at the security door. She looked at Carl Robbins. "Well? Let's get on with it."

Her patience was running thin. The sooner she could get out of Harbor Falls, the better. She hoped Jack had gone.

Carl Robbins nodded and set things in motion. He unlocked the vault, and they stepped inside the secure room. Quickly, they located box #352 and synchronized the keys in the locks. Within seconds, he had removed the box and handed it to Jasmine. It was heavier than she expected.

"There is a private room over here for you to go through the contents," he told her and motioned to the right. "Take your time. We'll be outside if you need us for anything."

Jasmine thanked Mr. Robbins and then looked at Art. "I'll

be fine. If I need any further help, I'll be sure and call. Thank you for your information."

Art nodded, shook her hand, and left.

Jasmine moved into the room, and Mr. Robbins shut the door behind her.

She placed the box on the table, stood over it and paused, a thousand thoughts rolling through her head. What in the world had Ms. Leinie done?

Then she looked toward the door. Was Jack still there?

Suddenly lightheaded, she sat in the chair with a deep sigh —her chest heaving with unspent air, her heart pounding.

Chapter Three

J asmine, 1999

  The nice thing about marching band practice being held early in the morning was that we avoided the August heat. And luckily for me, practice was at the same time the football team had their early practice.

We marched on the old practice field, but I could see the guys warming up and stretching on the big field. By the time band practice was finished, the players were pretty much geared up and ready to rock. They always got a little punchy and show-offy when we walked by. So much so that when my girlfriends, Kate and Kiesha and I, walked around the track toward the high school, we got a good glimpse of hot, sweaty, teenage boys in tight practice pants.

Not that seventeen-year-old girls looked. Much.

NOT!

"Going to Homecoming?" Kate Patterson asked. I glanced at her and then toward the field. Searching.

I shrugged. "Not sure. No date. Yet. What about you?"

"Todd Manchester asked me. I haven't said yes or no."

"Oh." I contemplated what Kate and Todd would look like as a Homecoming couple. "You'll need a dress," I told her.

"I bet Jack asks you."

I searched through the mass of boys on the field. Couldn't find him. "I don't know. The subject hasn't come up. He's really into football, and you know how the coach is about girls."

Kate interjected. "But it's Homecoming! The football players are expected to have dates. That's the way it works."

Since I'd never took part in Homecoming before, I really didn't know.

Kiesha Owens stopped in her tracks and tugged at my arm. "You sayin' that boy ain't asked you to Homecoming yet?"

I rolled my eyes. "We've only gone out a few times, Kiesha. It's not like we're talking seriously or anything."

She was the one who rolled her eyes then. "The way you two snuggle up at your locker? Girl, I figured you'd be knocked up by now."

Kate gasped. "Kiesha! Don't go saying things like that. You know that's how rumors get started."

Kiesha stepped in front of me. "Well, it's true. You all hot and heavy all over him after Science class."

I laughed. "I am not. I—"

"Heads up!" Kate pushed us both backwards. A football came soaring over our heads as I stumbled backward. I watched as Jack flashed by and caught the ball, landing with an oomph on his side about five feet away.

"Man, that had to hurt," Kiesha muttered. "Asphalt leaves bad burns. And those tiny little black balls...."

I rushed to Jack's side. He groaned and looked up. "Sorry," he said. "But you were about to get beaned by the ball."

He was in pain, I could tell, but his eyes crinkled and his smile was broad. "You're crazy," I said.

"For you," he replied.

And I wanted to kiss him. Hard.

A KNOCK CAME AT THE SECURITY ROOM DOOR, AND Jasmine jolted. Carl Robbins' voice came through the door. "Everything okay, Ms. Walker?"

"Yes, yes. Just fine. I'd like another few minutes, please."

"Of course."

She hadn't considered that he was hanging around outside the door.

Jasmine looked at the box and then slid the top back off the box. At once, she gasped.

Cash. The box was filled to the brim with cash. There was a yellow envelope with her name on top. With shaking hands, she reached for it, undid the flap, and slipped a single sheet of folded paper out of its place.

Jasmine opened the letter. It was dated the second day of January, this year.

DEAR JASMINE,

It has been many years since we have talked but I want you to know I have never forgotten you. Having you grow up in my house was one of my greatest pleasures. You were a joy to be with, such a kind and caring soul. I have missed you very much over the years but feel hopeful that I gave you what you needed while you were here.

Jasmine, I don't want you to fret about leaving. You were a woman coming into your own. I do regret, though, not being able to tell you why I said the things I said that day in the kitchen. I said it because I love you. And I fear you took my words the wrong way. I know I could have worded things differently perhaps, but at any rate, I apologize. You'll never know how deeply I missed you after you were gone and how I wished I could take back and erase our last words together.

I have to confess I've been following you all these years. You didn't know it, but I attended your college graduation, and when you received your law degree, I was there, too. I celebrated at home when I learned you had passed the bar exam. You've worked hard, Jasmine, and I am ever so proud of you.

But that is only part of why I am writing this letter.

By now, you have probably noticed this safe deposit box is full of cash. Sort of unconventional, wouldn't you say? Most people keep their money in an account, but I didn't want to do that with the money you have found here.

Jasmine, for all the years I took in foster children, I lived simply. I had enough money to live on from my own inheritance. Over time, my parents, my husband, and others left things to me, and I either sold or invested. So, I didn't really need the money from the state to keep all the children, and every dime I earned, I stashed away over the years. Usually, I hid it in the house but as the amount grew, I cashed it in for larger bills and just put it here, in this box.

I suppose you'll have to pay some sort of inheritance tax on the money, but perhaps not if you really see my wishes through. Jasmine, this money came from the children, and I want you to put it back to good use for the children. I'd like the money to stay here in Harbor Falls, to help care for the children in Harbor Falls who most need help. And there are a lot of them.

Children like you were. Will you please help them?

You are smart, and I know you'll know what to do. I'm trusting you, Jasmine.

LOVE, MS. LEINIE

. . .

24

WITH A HEAVY SIGH, JASMINE LIFTED HER EYES FROM the letter, looked up, and stared at the stark white wall opposite her. "Oh, hell..." she whispered. Then without thinking much further, she stood and went to the door, pulled it open, and spotted Carl Robbins waiting near the entrance to the bank lobby.

"Mr. Robbins."

He turned. "Yes, Ms. Walker?"

She motioned for him to join her. "I need your help and have someone call Art Manchester. I need him too."

He nodded, and she went back into the room and stood staring at the money until Carl entered. She still held the letter in her hand.

Carl stepped up to the table, looked at the box, and said, "Wow."

She nodded her agreement. "That's definitely not a recipe box."

"No. No, it's not." He flipped through the pack of bills on top. "All hundreds," he said.

"Yep. I guess we need to count it," she said.

"We'll have someone here at the bank do it for you."

That sounded logical. "Yes. But let's wait for Art. I have a feeling I'm going to need some advice."

She glanced again at her watch. *And I'm probably not going to get back to Atlanta tonight.*

JACK TOLD SAM TO TAKE THE TRUCK HOME. NO WAY was he budging from the bank until he saw Jasmine walk back out that hallway and into the lobby. And there was no way *in hell* he was letting her leave the bank until he'd talked with her.

Dammit.

Fifteen years just flew by in a minute, and suddenly his

heart was racing as it had when he was seventeen and kissed her lips for the very first time.

Where was she?

Felt like he'd waited for hours already. Was there a back exit?

He rose. Hell.

Cam Parker rounded a corner from behind the teller windows. "Hey, Jack," he said. "Thanks for sticking around. I got caught up in a meeting off-site."

Jack figured the meeting was with a doughnut and coffee at Sidney's bakery on the other side of the block. Cam reached out to shake Jack's hand. "Let's go into my office, and we'll get the details about the estate and your project."

Heels clicked on the hard tile floor. Distracted, Jack turned his gaze toward the sound. He lifted a finger. "One minute, Cam."

He waited only another second, maybe two. Then voices echoed in the hallway, and the heels clicked louder.

Jack started toward the entrance to the hallway. "Cam, I may have to postpone..."

Jasmine moved gracefully down the hall, walking between the two men. Tall and thin and beautiful, dressed in a dark suit, the skirt hitting her just above the knees, her long legs punctuated with black heels, a scarlet, low-cut blouse peeking out between the lapels of her jacket—she commanded a presence that hadn't struck him earlier.

Earlier, he was simply captured by her being there. Now, he was captivated by the stunning woman she had grown into.

He glanced down at himself. He looked like he'd just stepped off the farm.

Well, he had.

The three were chatting intensely, and he was actually glad of that. He was standing before her before she realized he was there.

He halted.

They stopped short.

Jasmine looked straight into his eyes. Her face was expressionless. Like she was wearing her best lawyer face. But just beneath the surface, he sensed something else.

"Jack," she breathed. "You're still here?"

He glanced at both men, then back at her. "Yes. I waited."

"For me?"

He resisted a chuckle. "Yes, Jasmine. I waited for you. When you're finished here, could we talk? I promise, just a few minutes. To catch up. That is, if you can spare the time...."

He watched her big eyes blink once, twice. Her eyelashes were heavenly long, fringing her large brown eyes. They looked even bigger today than when they were kids. He'd stared into them too many times, that was for sure.

"Jasmine?"

She exhaled and then nodded. "Of course, Jack." Then she turned to the men. "Mr. Robbins, I'll see you in the morning, and Art, as soon as I decide, I'll be in touch."

Both men nodded their agreement and faced away. In the next instant, Jack squared himself in front of Jasmine. "You're staying in Harbor Falls?"

She sighed, and her shoulders noticeably dropped. "I guess I am. For tonight, anyway."

Inside, Jack's heart was about to burst. "Have you had lunch?"

Jasmine shook her head. "No."

"Good. Let's find a bite to eat and then see if Suzie has a room at Sweet Hart Inn."

Chapter Four

"So, Jack, what *have* you been doing all these years?"

Jack fiddled with his napkin, glanced off, and then back again into Jasmine's eyes. He could get lost in the depths, no doubt about that. Her eyes had always drawn him in, as if pulled directly into her soul. At this moment, he honestly didn't know how to answer her question, because as of a few minutes ago, when their gazes connected again, it was like the last fifteen years of this life had not even existed.

Suddenly, he was eighteen again and staring into her eyes across a pizza and Coke on a late Friday afternoon.

"Working mostly. You?"

Jasmine nodded. Jack glanced around the restaurant again. Why in hell hadn't he suggested something nicer? Mario's Subs was an Old Harbor Falls classic, but hell, he could have done better than this. He wasn't eighteen anymore.

After all, this was Jasmine.

"I guess I could say the same," she said. "School and then work. That's been my life."

Jack looked back into her face. "I can honestly say I have

29

done little else, either. Nothing exciting here." He laughed, and Jasmine smiled.

God, he loved that smile.

"I didn't finish up at the university."

Her eyes widened. "Oh? What happened?"

Jack shrugged. "I stayed a year and a half. Sam graduated and came home. He had a brainchild over the summer to start Haven's Hill Nursery—that's our business—and I was into it, too. You know, landscaping, selling flowers and trees and shrubs, and so on. Once the business got off the ground, I decided not to go back to school. Sam needed me. It's been good for us the past few years."

Jasmine's gaze held the connection. "That's fabulous, Jack. Your own business..." She let her words trail off, and Jack wondered what she was thinking. Did she see a loser sitting in front of her who dropped out of college? A farm boy?

He looked her over again. Expensive clothes. She'd done well for herself.

"I went to Georgia State," she said, and then added almost apologetically, "for seven years."

"Seven? Wow. Music?"

"No. Law. I'm an attorney."

Shit. If he had thought he was out of her league earlier, he knew it now. "Sounds important."

Shrugging, she said, "I think so. Some may not, but I love what I do. I fight for the rights of children and families. I'm a children's advocate attorney."

Something tickled at the back burners of his brain. Children. They talked about having children. How many had they said they wanted? Four? Five?

"Those children are fortunate to have you," he said.

She was the one to glance off this time. "Actually, it's my privilege."

Silence twittered about them.

"Do you have children, Jasmine?" He had to know. It almost pained him to ask, but he had to. Because if she had children, then probably she had a husband....

Her gaze landed square on his. "No," she said. "No children. I've never really had a serious relationship since..." She stopped and looked at the table. Toyed with her fork. Paused. "Children just don't seem to be in the cards for me, but maybe this way is better. I can help so many more." And then, glancing up, she added, "What about you, Jack?"

He echoed her words. "No. No children."

"Married?"

"No. Not married."

"Me either," she said.

It seemed then that both of them sighed. Jack realized he'd barely touched his sandwich. Jasmine took another bite of her salad. Finally, he mustered up enough courage to reach out and touch her hand resting on the table.

"Jasmine." He cleared his throat.

She stopped chewing, glanced at their touching hands, and then looked up into his eyes.

Jack stumbled over his next words. "I just... Oh hell. I have to say this. I'm not sure why you are here, what your plans are... But I need some time with you. To catch up. I don't want to do that over a meatball sub and salad. And I don't want you to leave until we've had time to talk."

He paused and watched her face. "Jasmine, we really need to talk."

She finished chewing her salad and swallowed. "What are you saying, Jack?"

Before he lost his nerve, he blurted out, "Drive me to my house. I sent Sam back to the farm earlier with my truck. We can catch up in private. On the way, I'll call Suzie to see if she has a room for you tonight at the inn."

The look she gave him then was akin to fight or flight , and he wasn't certain which direction she was going to take. He half expected her to flee, the way she had years earlier.

But she surprised him. Her fingers curled around his palm. "Jack. I think that's a great idea."

———

THE INSIDE OF JASMINE'S AUDI shrank incredibly the moment Jack got in and sat in the passenger seat. His presence took up every inch of space, and his essence held captive every one of her senses. She couldn't breathe. He sucked the air out of her lungs. Every nerve ending under her skin was on high alert. The air tasted of the scent of male. And all she could hear was the beating of her heart in her chest.

Or was it his?

No, it was hers. The blood pounded in her ears.

This was Jack. Beside her. Crowding into her private space. Her bubble, as her kids would sometimes say.

She liked it. Somehow, it all felt incredibly warm and safe and... Right.

"I'm looking forward to seeing your place," she told him, barely getting the words out. She kept her eyes on the narrow Harbor Falls street in front of her. "Is it near your parents' farm? Otherwise, you'll need to show me the way."

Jack watched her from the side. The heat of his stare hit her cheeks. She hoped to hell and back she wasn't blushing. He used to tease her when her cheeks flamed. Her skin was light enough that a rosy glow showed through her darker complexion. Right now, she felt on fire, and she hoped she wasn't showing it.

How long had it been since she'd felt flushed?

Years. Maybe.

"Just head to the farm. When we get close, there's an extra

turn or two. I'll let you know. I have a small piece of land near the back, close to the lake."

Jasmine glanced his way. "Oh?"

She looked at him long enough to see his gaze narrow and a slight grin break across his lips. "Yes, Jazzy. I built my house on our spot."

At that moment, Jasmine's heart catapulted. She nodded. "Then I'm pretty sure I know the way."

JASMINE, 1999

The place I felt the most secure, the most me, was in Jack's arms. And when he was kissing me, I didn't have a care in the world. Everything else went away.

Who I am.

How I grew up.

None of it mattered. To me or to Jack. And tonight, lying in his arms in the bed of his pickup truck, wrapped up in a couple of sleeping bags to keep us warm, and staring up at the stars, everything was perfect.

Jack knew the stars and the constellations. *There's you, Gemini,* he'd say and point to constellation. *And there's me, Aquarius. One day I'm going to shoot across the sky and be with you forever. I'd cross the sky for you, Jazzy,* he'd say. *I love you that much.*

Growing up in town, I was used to noise at night—cars, people talking, music—especially before I went to Ms. Leinie's. My father's house was small and across the street from a bar. Not to mention the train that ran through my part of town in the night. I learned to ignore the sounds so I could sleep at an early age. Ms. Leinie's was different, but there were other noises. The old house creaked with the wind, her cats running and playing in the night, a thundering herd on the

33

old hardwood. Her dogs barking occasionally from their preferred sleeping spots.

But this was real quiet, and I loved it out there. Our favorite spot—tucked away on the backside of Jack's parents' farm, the last bit of flat land before the foothills of the mountains and close enough to the lake you could hear water lapping the shore.

Jack leaned over, propping his head on an elbow, and peered into my eyes. The light was on in the truck's cab, lending a small glow over us through the back window. His eyes twinkled in the moonlight as he traced my face with his forefinger.

His sexy smile, that half-curled lip, and those dreamy chocolate brown eyes....

Mine. All mine.

His light touch sent a tremor of need through me. A need that only he sparked. I'd never been with a boy before sexually. Not until Jack. And I never wanted to be with another boy again. *I can't imagine ever feeling the way I do for anyone else.*

Ever.

Leaning in, he captured my lips. Rolling slightly over me, he groaned. "As soon as we get out of college," he said softly, "we're going to have babies. Lots of babies. Just so you know."

I giggled. He'd said things like that before. I knew Jack wanted a family. If he could get by without going to college and move straight into work and being a family man, he wouldn't have minded. But college was something his parents insisted on.

"After graduate school," I reminded him. "Then we can talk."

He frowned. "That's at least five years."

"We're only eighteen, Jack!"

Grinning, he leaned forward and caught my lips in a kiss.

"I know. I am impatient. All I can think of when making love with you is making beautiful babies that look just like you."

"Jack! Really?" I laughed.

"It's true," he said. "You will make beautiful babies."

"We will." I marveled at the wonder of it all. How many other eighteen-year-old men wanted babies? Thought about babies? Most were trying hard not to make them. "You're insane," I added.

"I'm horny."

Well, there was that. "Now you're normal."

"God, I want you again, Jazzy."

I giggled. We shouldn't. I didn't care.

Jack was mine. I was his.

And we were still naked in the sleeping bags.

"We still have a little time," I whispered, rising to meet his lips and kiss him back.

He shifted lower to my chest, his mouth catching a nipple and sucking. The sensation zinged between my legs. Hot. I was already hot for him.

"Jack," I breathed. "Lower."

Chapter Five

J asmine stared out from the back deck of Jack's house, her gaze fixed on the lapping waters of Falls Lake several yards in front of her, and the foothills of the mountains in the distance. Her eyes scanned the horizon, traveling east to west and back again, taking in things she hadn't seen in a very long time.

The old lodge sat across the way, nestled in Harbor Falls' own mountain, its façade overlooking the lake. But it didn't look old anymore. Someone must have bought it and fixed it up. She remembered driving up there with friends when she was in high school, a case of beer in tow, and sleeping off a little buzz on the deck. They hadn't done it often—she had always felt guilty lying to Ms. Leinie about where she was spending the night.

She took a deep breath and sighed. Ms. Leinie. What was she going to do about the estate?

She shook off that thought. "I'll think about that later," she muttered. Right now, other thoughts occupied her brain. Like Jack, and this incredible house he had built on 'their spot.'

It was all too beautiful. The picturesque landscape, the log home, and that it was right there—in the place where they had spent many a night dreaming of the future.

Unexpectedly, her eyes stung.

"I put our lunches in the refrigerator for later."

Jasmine turned at Jack's words to see him coming out the French doors leading onto the deck. She looked at him, caught his eyes. He halted, holding the connection between them. The expression on his face went from smiling to serious in a flash. And she realized the emotion she was feeling was playing all over hers, leaving nothing to speculation.

Jack stepped closer. "Jazzy..." he whispered. Reaching up, he caught a strand of her hair between his fingers. That touch, so close to her cheek, was the beginning of her unraveling. "Are you okay?" he added.

She nodded and then glanced about. "Yes. Jack, this is all so beautiful."

"You are beautiful."

Her heart ached. Shaking her head, she said. "You never married, Jack. Why? I'm sure a wife would have enjoyed this beautiful place."

Jack sighed. "No one was ever right, Jazzy. Not after you."

"But we were so young, so...wrong," she countered.

He took another step closer. "No." His voice softened. "We were so right."

Jack leaned in and brushed his lips across hers. A long-dormant curl of desire burst up and sprinted through her body, from her lips, to her heart, to her soul. At that moment, all she wanted was to be as close to Jack as she could possibly get.

But she pushed back.

Her hands went to his chest, and she applied a little pressure while she stepped away. Her gaze met his, and her heart swelled. He searched her eyes.

"Jack," she said softly, "as much as I am overcome by this moment, I think we need to step back a bit."

His hands went to his sides. "Jazzy. I'm so sorry. I got carried away and—"

She stopped him with a forefinger on his lips. "No, don't. I could just as easily get carried away here myself, but I don't think that's what we need right now."

He stared at her a little longer and then agreed. "Okay. You're not running?"

She thought about that for a second. Of course, he would expect her to run. Right?

Shaking her head, she replied, "No, Jack. Not running. It's time for me to face up to the past. Can we talk about what happened fifteen years ago?"

JASMINE, 1999

Looking over my shoulder, I glance back to Ms. Leinie's house, knowing this was the last time I would see her, or the house that I practically grew up in, for the rest of my life. A bittersweet sensation fluttered in my belly, making me slow my steps. I was ever so grateful for the life I lived with Ms. Leinie, and everything she provided me, but also apprehensive about the future, and a little melancholy about the past.

I longed for a life away from here, where I could get lost in the crowd and not stand out. Not be different. I couldn't wait to experience college, to spread my wings, try new things, find out who I really was—without the barriers of this small town, where I never really fit in.

But at what price?

I was sacrificing a lot. I knew that. Everything. I owed Ms. Leinie my life. I was doomed to fend for myself after my father was incarcerated, my mother dead in the cemetery. I was a moody, backward, and defiant eleven-year-old child who didn't understand why she'd been dealt the hand of being born to an odd couple—a black woman who eventually committed suicide and an alcoholic white man.

But it was time to move on. Deep in my heart, I knew it was time for me to do so, and what was about to happen next was best for everyone involved.

Wearing my white graduation dress, my heavy orange backpack slung over my shoulder, I strolled down the sidewalk leading downtown and to Harbor Falls High, my thoughts scattered. I had to rein them in before I reached the school. This was an important night in so many ways.

One door closed. Another opened?

Or will that one slam in my face, too?

I sneaked around to the back of the school, crossed the track and the marching band practice field, and then headed toward the baseball field dugouts. I'd left the house early to give myself a little time, but must have dawdled more than I thought. Glancing at my watch, I realized I needed to get a move on. Graduates were supposed to be in the gym in fifteen minutes to practice our line-up and procession one more time before they opened the doors for parents and families.

Quickly, I stashed the backpack beneath the bench seat in the dugout, pushing it far back enough to where it wouldn't easily be seen. Glancing up, I noticed the angle of the security light. It would give me just enough light to sneak back and retrieve the bag much later, in the dark.

I hurried off toward the back gym door, rounded the football bleachers, and was thinking about the next few hours when I was stopped short.

"Jazzy!"

"Oh, my God!" My hands went to my throat. "Jack!"

"I'm so sorry. I didn't mean to scare you, honey!"

I blew out a breath. "No, sorry. I was just thinking. Not paying attention."

"Come here." He tugged both of my hands and pulled me back into the shadows under the bleachers. He must have noticed my frantic glance at the gym door. "For just a minute. I know we need to go."

I nodded. "Okay."

He pulled me closer and wrapped his arms around me. I melted into his chest and tried not to cry. His heartbeat was solid against me, and he was so warm. So safe. Mine.

"I love you, Jazzy," he whispered into my hair.

"I love you back."

I felt the deep sigh escape his lungs as we held each other for a moment to last a lifetime. Then Jack pulled back, cupped my face in his hands, kissed me on the end of my nose, and said, "I'll meet you behind the Town Hall at ten-thirty. Watch for my truck. I can't wait."

I nodded and watched him walk away.

JACK STUDIED JASMINE'S FACE. THIS DAY HAD BEEN A whirlwind and it was barely afternoon. This morning, he'd had no idea that the love of his life, gone for over fifteen years, would walk right back into it. The surreality of that fact was almost more than he could comprehend. But Jasmine was here, in the flesh, standing on his deck right in front of him. It was a scene he had pictured in his mind repeatedly throughout the years. In his dreams, however, he would carry her upstairs and make slow, delicious love to her, all night long.

That would not happen today. Tonight.

He took a deep breath. There was no way he was going to let her slip through his fingers this time, though.

"Let's go inside and sit down. That breeze sure is brisk coming off the lake."

She nodded, and he took her elbow, leading her into the great room. He closed the French doors behind them. She sat on the sofa, and he followed, sitting a respectable few inches away. Right now, he wasn't sure he trusted himself.

"Did you call this Suzie at the inn?" she asked.

Jack nodded. "I did. They are full. She apologized profusely and recommended another B&B in Asheville. I can call them if you like."

Her mouth drew up into a bow; her brows knit. It was a funny little expression he remembered from when they were kids, and it almost made him giddy-happy inside at the remembrance.

"I don't know. I suppose I don't have a choice," she said. "Asheville is two hours away though, right?"

"Yes. Not very convenient."

"But I suppose I'll have to though.

"Well, maybe not. If you want to take it, I have a spare room." Her eyes widened, and he put up his hands in self-defense. "Hey, I'll be a good boy," he added.

Jasmine's face relaxed. "I don't know, Jack. I'm not sure that is a good id—"

"You don't want to drive to Asheville tonight and back again tomorrow."

She bit her lip. "No, I really don't."

"Besides, we can continue to catch up." That's when he clasped her hands and pulled them onto his lap and said, "Jasmine, stay. I promise to give you space. I have some sweats and a T-shirt you can sleep in, and we can do a load of laundry tonight."

"Jack, that is generous, but I don't want to put you out..."

"Not putting me out. Besides, if you stay, it will be good

for me. I'll have the best night of sleep I've had in fifteen years."

Her gaze narrowed. "Why is that?"

"Because you're back home, and I know you are safe."

At that, she burst into tears.

JASMINE WASN'T SURE WHAT WAS WRONG WITH HER. She wasn't an emotional person. Law school had drilled that out of her. She'd learned to disconnect herself from the situation and view it for what it was—just the facts, ma'am. She'd had to harden her heart working with the children—on the outside, at least—but inside, she bled with sorrow and sympathy for them. She'd lost many a night's sleep over the children she served. They were a part of her life, every case she took on, but she kept the families at arm's length. Being impartial was a way of life for her.

But once she'd stepped back into Harbor Falls, once she'd seen Jack, that stoic personality she prided herself on professionally, and sometimes personally, crumbled.

"Jazzy?"

Jack's gaze caught hers, his eyes pleading. "Are you okay?"

Fifteen years of grief spilled forward. "Jack, I am so sorry!"

"For what?"

For what? How can he ask that? "For graduation night! For leaving you there waiting for me behind the Town Hall. No explanation. Nothing. I don't know how you could ever forgive me!"

"Ah, Jazzy...."

Jack had her in his arms within seconds. She was crying uncontrollably, wetting his shirt with her tears. He held her, cooed in her ear, and threaded his fingers through her hair. She didn't know what to do other than just let him hold her.

"Jazzy," he whispered, "we were young."

"Young and scared," she echoed back.

"I wasn't scared. I was in love."

Jasmine pulled back and looked him square in the eyes. "I was scared."

He ran a knuckle under her eyes, brushing away the tears. She sucked in two quick breaths, and then exhaled long. "I was scared, Jack," she whispered. "I was pregnant."

Chapter Six

J ack felt the blood drain from his face. "Pregnant?"

He watched Jasmine's head dip and nod. "Yes."

Unable to sit, he jerked back and up off the couch, raking his fingers through his hair, and paced in front of the fireplace.

He'd not been angry at Jasmine—not for a long time. Oh, when she didn't show up that night after graduation, and when he'd stopped by Ms. Leinie's the next day and had learned she'd run off to go live with her aunt in Atlanta, leaving a note behind for Ms. Leinie on her bed—nothing for him—he'd been plenty angry for weeks.

And sad. Depressed.

But pregnant?

He whirled back. Jasmine's face looked like a mess, eyes swollen, cheeks red and damp. "Why? Jasmine, why didn't you tell me?" A million questions circled his brain. "I would have helped. Taken care of you. I deserved to know."

"I know, Jack. I know. But—"

"But what? There is no 'but' Jazzy. We were pregnant. Not

just you. We. I had a right to know. To raise..." He stopped short. "God, Jasmine. Where is the baby? Child?"

She stood. "Jack, I haven't thought about this in years. I— I am feeling all kinds of things I've pushed deep inside me. Suddenly it's all..." She hiccupped a little and swiped her eyes. "I feel like I'm coming apart at the seams...and I don't know how to—"

"Jazzy. The baby. Tell me."

She gulped. "How— How do I tell...?"

Pain and anguish ripped through Jack's chest. He rushed forward and grasped both of her upper arms. "Hell, Jasmine. What did you do? Where is our child?"

"Dead!" The word burst from her mouth, and Jack bolted backwards. Jasmine turned, stumbled toward the table where she'd left her purse and keys earlier, and snatched them up. Spinning back, she faced Jack for a moment, breathing in and out quick, sharp breaths. "He was stillborn. Our baby somehow died inside of me, Jack. I lived with my aunt, but she could barely take care of herself, let alone a pregnant teenage girl. I didn't get the proper prenatal care, and there was a problem. I gave birth to a dead baby boy. Something about his heart. And it was the hardest thing I have ever had to go through in all of my life."

She turned then and headed for the front door. All Jack could do was stand there and watch her go, until sudden grief for a lost child he would never know overtook him, and he dropped to his knees.

JASMINE GOT IN HER CAR AND DROVE. No destination in mind, she just needed to get away. Think. Pull herself together. What she hated about leaving more than anything was that she was leaving Jack. Again. But she hadn't been prepared to have that full discussion. And the emotion that had welled up inside of her took her totally by surprise.

Pull yourself together, Jasmine.

The steady drone of tires on pavement slowed the racing cadence of her heart. Calmed her. Somewhat. Inside, she was a mess, and that was something she was not used to.

Cool, calm and collected. That's her.

"Not today," she muttered.

She drove straight through Harbor Falls, the few stoplights and lower speed limits forcing her to pace herself. She kept going until she crossed the railroad tracks and turned off Main Street and realized she knew exactly where she was going.

Her foot eased off the accelerator, and her car slowed as she approached 102 East Court Street. Once there, she pulled over and parked. For several long moments, she stared at the decaying front porch, the rotting steps, and the tattered screen door leading inside. A gray cat stretched and stalked across the porch. Its presence made her wonder if her original assumption, that the house was abandoned, was indeed correct.

In her mind's eye, she saw the screen door ease open and her father step out on the porch, white T-shirt, jeans, taking a drag off a cigarette. He leaned against the porch baluster and exhaled a stream of smoke. His gaze surveyed his surroundings.

JASMINE, 1989

I was sitting in the back of a police cruiser. By myself. Sitting up straight on the cold, hard bench seat, studying the pieces of metal that separated the back seat from the front. The doors were locked, and I couldn't get out. I'd tried. Blue and red lights swirled above the car, casting their reflection against the dirty, gray shingles of my house. I'd stopped crying, but my eyes were still blurry, my cheeks tight from drying tears and snot.

My daddy was on the porch. Drunk. Arguing with the policeman. Then I watched him sit on the steps, hanging his head in his hands.

A stranger had roused me from my bed. A woman. She was outside the car now, standing right beside the door where I was sitting, talking to another policeman. I didn't know where Mommy was.

She'd tucked me in with a story and a song hours earlier. Daddy wasn't home from work yet. But sometimes Daddy didn't come home from work at all until the next morning, when he'd stumble in about the time I was eating breakfast, getting ready for school. I knew I had to hurry to get out of the bathroom on those days, when he wasn't there yet, because he'd want the shower as soon as he stepped in the door. He'd clean up, drink a couple of cups of coffee that Mommy had made for him, and then head out to work again.

I was used to it.

But it didn't happen that way today. Something was wrong.

A man in a black car pulled up, got out, and went to the porch. He talked to my daddy and the police and then went inside. He looked important. I just wanted to know where Mommy was.

The woman outside tapped on the window. "You okay, honey?" she said.

I nodded. Wanted to cry again. Didn't.

I held it in. *Be strong, Jasmine. Be a strong girl.* Mommy said those words tonight. *I love you.*

The man from the black car came out and stood on the porch. He crooked his finger at some other men. They pulled a long bed thing out of the back of the black car and rolled it into the house. My heart kicked inside my chest. I didn't know why; it just did. And over the next few minutes, my life went into slow motion. The things happening in front me moved in reverse time-warp speed. And a small, but growing voice inside of me said, "There is nothing you can do about this, Jasmine." *Be strong, girl. Be strong.*

The bed and the men came out the front door. They lifted it down the porch steps. And my mommy's arm slipped out from under the sheet and hung off the side.

I screamed and beat at the metal between the seats until my palm was bloody.

JACK TURNED THE CORNER FROM MAIN AND COURT and immediately spotted Jasmine's car. He'd driven all over town and hadn't found her—finally giving up, assuming she'd headed back to Atlanta—and then stopped by the construction site to check on a few things.

The last person he expected to see in this part of town was Jasmine.

His heart heavy, feeling the same sort of confusion, he'd felt years earlier, he parked in front of the old Belk's Bar. He was relieved to have found her, and his heart lightened a bit. But was she ready to see him after the scene at his house? As he crossed the street, he watched her sitting on the steps of an old house, leaning against a post, staring out into space.

Slowly, he approached. She turned and looked his way. She'd been crying but wasn't now. That was good. Still, he moved with caution, carefully navigating both the deteriorating steps and their rickety relationship.

Her gaze followed him as he settled in facing her. A small space of silence separated them.

"I lived here for eleven years," she started, glancing toward the partially open door. "I was relatively happy. I knew nothing else but what our life was. I thought it was normal. It wasn't. I didn't know any better until I got to Ms. Leinie's, and that was a change, for sure."

She stopped, and Jack let the silence between them add to the conversation.

She heaved a sigh. "Mommy killed herself. She took a lot of pills and went to sleep. I guess she knew our life wasn't normal. I wish she had been stronger." She looked at him. "That's why I had to be strong, you know? I didn't want to end up like my mommy."

He nodded. Understanding.

"The next three years went downhill. I tried to take care of the house, go to school, make the coffee for Daddy. I tried. We hid it well that he wasn't there most of the time, and I was way too young to be taking on all of that responsibility. I even made sure the electric bill was paid because Daddy often forgot. I'd sneak money out of his wallet, a few dollars at a time, and stash them away until I had enough to walk down to the bank and pay the bill. It got so they knew I was coming, eventually, and it was enough to keep the lights and heat turned on. I think they took pity on me."

She looked at Jack, her gaze playing over his face. He felt her need for him to understand, because they'd never gone this deep into Jasmine's past, before this. And it explained so much.

"But when I turned eleven, it wasn't enough. One week in January, Daddy didn't come home. I went to school and back every day, and he wasn't there. Seven days. Groceries were almost gone. I didn't have any money. And they turned off the heat. I told my teacher, finally, when she asked why I was so tired. How can you sleep when you are freezing and hungry? The next day I went to Ms. Leinie's."

"Oh, Jazzy."

"And two years after that, my dad when to prison. To tell

you the truth, I'm not even sure why. No one really talked to me about it. I visited him once. Ms. Leinie took me on a family day. It didn't go well, and I never wanted to go back. I think he got out a few years ago. I haven't heard from him."

"You don't know where he is?"

"I don't. And it is okay."

Her life had been hard. So much harder than his. He'd always known that, but as kids, what do you really comprehend? Now, his soul ached for her.

He studied her face. Her demeanor. She looked at ease, comfortable, sitting there. A mixture perhaps, defeated and resolved at the same time. He wasn't sure which. She just appeared calm.

Acceptance. That was it. Perhaps.

"I went to law school to help the children. I lived what they live. Thank God for Ms. Leinie. And to think I left and never talked to her again. And now she's left me all of this money, and I need to figure out what to do—"

"She knew you loved her."

Jasmine peered into his eyes. "Oh?"

He nodded. "We'd talk about you from time to time."

Her face screwed into a small puzzle. "I had no clue."

"No, you wouldn't have."

She closed her eyes. "Touché."

An expectant silence fell between them, then Jasmine added, "Ms. Leinie was right."

"About what?"

She shifted, angling toward him. "I guess your parents probably knew about my family. I guess the whole town did. It was more than that I was a bi-racial child; it was that my daddy was white trash and in prison, and my mommy was a black woman who must have had something really wrong with her to kill herself. Why would your parents want you to be married to me?"

"Jazzy…" Jack eased closer.

She shook her head and put a hand up. Jack sat still.

"It's okay. I understand it all now. I probably would have done the same thing if I were in their shoes. But when you are eighteen and in love, and someone tells you that you are living a pipe dream, you don't hear what they are actually saying. All you hear are the rumblings of your past spurting up to hurt your heart. The snickers from kids in the lunch line. The sad looks from parents as they herded their kids away. It all came back when Ms. Leinie was trying to talk candidly with me. I shouldn't have said the awful things I said to her."

Jack exhaled and reached for her hand.

"She was just trying to warn me, protect my heart. And I had to go get all bitchy on her. And then when I did, I knew I had to leave there as soon as possible because I felt so bad."

"You never apologized?"

"No."

"But she never forgot you, did she? And evidently she forgave you. Otherwise, you wouldn't be here today."

She nodded, glancing off. Eyes closed.

Jack eased out a long breath. "Jasmine, I'm sorry I yelled at you earlier. My God, I was in shock."

Her eyes flashed open. For the longest moment she held his gaze, and then whispered, "Jack, I pushed that pain away fifteen years ago. I had to, so I could move on and do what I had to do. I didn't keep it from you on purpose. The baby dying part, anyway. When I left, I figured I'd write or call you and tell you about the baby when I was settled in with my aunt. I thought, maybe, me getting out of Harbor Falls would be the best thing. Especially after Ms. Leinie…" She paused and didn't finish. "But one thing led to another, and by the time the problem happened with the baby, it was too late. So, I just did it all. Alone. And then I let it go."

Oh, Jazzy. If I could only turn back time. "I wish I had been there for you."

"I wish that too." An awkward pause settled between them. "He was a boy, Jack," she added softly.

Something gripped his throat. A son. *Oh, God.* "Jasmine, I don't want to bring back any pain for you, but...did you see him? Hold him?"

She sniffled and nodded. "For a while. They let me hold him. He had the darkest hair. I couldn't stop touching it, fiddling with it. He was a beautiful child, Jack. And then I had to give him back, let him go."

"Did you? Really? Let it go?"

Her eyes welled up, tears spilled over. "No," she said softly. "No."

Jack's eyes stung. He scooted across the porch step and pulled her into his arms. She rested her head on his shoulder and sighed, then sobbed a little. "Sh... I have you now, Jazzy. I'm here now."

She clutched at his back and held him tight. "Thank you, Jack. I'm glad you know now. I'm so sorry about everything."

After a moment, she pulled away, closed her eyes, and distanced herself from him. She leaned her head back against the post, her face pointing skyward. She breathed deeply, and Jack watched her chest expand, and her shoulders relax a little as she exhaled. They sat there for a while in silence.

Finally, she sat up. "How did you find me? I never told you where I lived before I came to Ms. Leinie's."

"By accident, actually. Not that I wasn't looking for you. I was. But I was on my way to check on the construction site—Ms. Leinie's project."

Her gaze narrowed. "Ms. Leinie's project?"

He nodded. "Yes. Would you like to see?"

Chapter Seven

Jasmine stepped down from the passenger side of Jack's four-wheel-drive pickup truck. They hadn't traveled far down Court Street, perhaps six or seven blocks from where Jasmine's house sat, when he pulled off the road and into a construction site. As Jasmine glanced about, surveying the buildings in front of her and across the street, she tried to remember what business sat on that spot years earlier.

"This was the old Laundrymat building," Jack said, rounding the front of the truck.

Jasmine snapped her fingers. "That's right! I spent many a Saturday evening here with Mommy while she did the wash. She liked to go on Saturday night because not as many people were there, and she could use more than one washer." She turned about. "Then that means that the..." She spotted the small square building with the crooked and slanted roof. "There. The doughnut shop was over there." She pointed across the street.

"Yes, it was."

She crossed her arms over her chest and smiled at the

memory. "Mr. Jimmy used to leave the back door open." She giggled. "Mommy would let me walk over before dark, because he had day-old doughnuts he would give us for our Sunday morning breakfast. Mama would warm those in the oven and serve them with ice-cold milk. I never tasted anything so good in my life."

She glanced at Jack, who was smiling at her.

"Mr. Jimmy was busy getting things ready for the morning. He opened real early, before the chickens got up, he used to say." The memory felt good, and her heart opened. "He'd bag up a dozen glazed for Mommy, and he'd give me a small bag of donut holes I could have for a snack that night. Then he'd walk me back across the street."

She stood there, staring at the old shop. A strong sense of the past, of home, neighborhood and community, overcame her. She looked at Jack. "I guess growing up on the wrong side of the tracks could still be a good thing, at times."

Jack reached up to smooth a stray curl out of her face. "It's good to see you smile again, Jasmine."

Nodding, she said, "Thanks, Jack. It feels good. I swear I've run the gamut of emotions today." Then she broke the connection between them and stepped toward the building under construction. "So, is this Ms. Leinie's project?"

"It is."

She kept walking, up a couple of steps and through a doorway. The building was framed up, two-by-fours showing like a skeleton, with no roof yet. Turning back, she asked, "What is it?"

Jack shrugged. Shoving his hands into his pockets, he joined her inside. "Right now, it's just a building, although I am pretty sure Ms. Leinie had something in mind. She just didn't share it."

"I don't understand."

He laughed. "Me either. She came to me a few months ago

and said, "Jack Ackerman, I want you to build me a building. I have the plans and the money. I just need a man to do the job, and I believe you are the right man."

Amazed, Jasmine looked back and perused the structure, wandering further into the room. "I'm sure she had a plan."

"Oh, I'm positive she did. She did say something once like, 'It's for the kids.'"

For the kids? "What happens now that she's gone?"

"That's why I was at the bank this morning. To go over how to continue the work according to the plans left in Ms. Leinie's will."

Swinging about, she stared at Jack. "That's why I was at the bank this morning." She thought of the money in the safe deposit box and the letter. *For the kids.* "Ms. Leinie left some of her estate to me."

Jack held her gaze. "She did?"

Jasmine nodded. Suddenly, it was all coming together. "Yeah. Oh goodness, Jack. Ms. Leinie had a plan, all right, but not only for the kids. I mean, I believe it *is* for the kids, because of her big heart—but it's also about something else."

Stepping forward, Jack said, "Such as?"

"It's about us, Jack. You and me."

"Us?"

"Getting us back together. Or, at least, giving us a second chance to consider it."

Jack said nothing. A long moment passed, and Jasmine's heart froze. Why did she say that out loud? Why couldn't she have just kept that thought to herself? She turned away and started out of the building toward the truck.

"Jasmine, wait." Jack touched her elbow. "You may be right. I was just thinking."

Jasmine looked at him and chuckled. "But that's all ridiculous, right? We're older and wiser now. Grown up. What we had was puppy love. That's gone now. Besides, we have different lives, and meshing them would be, well—"

She paused.

Jack waited. "Well, what?"

"Well, ridiculous."

But her eyes told a different story than her words. Jack studied her, and she knew he knew how she really felt. He could always read Jasmine like a book, and the confusion in her eyes apparently spoke volumes. "You don't mean that."

She blinked and took a few more steps away, then turned. "I think I'd like to walk back to my car. It's only a few blocks, and I need to clear my head."

Jack nodded. "Okay, and then...?"

Her chest heaved with a deep inhale, and then her words escaped on a breath. "I don't know."

"It's too late to go back to Atlanta."

"I'm not. I have a meeting in the morning."

"Then come back to the house. Stay the night. I'll give you all the space you need."

Her shoulders dropped. Did she really have a choice? "Okay. I won't be a bother. I'll pick up a few things somewhere, and then I'll be on up. But don't worry if I'm not there right away. Take your time going home. This has been quite a day, and I need some time to just..."

"Think?"

"Yes."

He knew what she meant. Some downtime would be good for him, too. "I'll see you when I see you."

She nodded and headed down the street.

THE WINDING DRIVE UP TO MS. LEINIE'S HOUSE WAS not as steep as she remembered. This was a typical case of having grown up in a place that seemed so huge when you were a child, but when you revisited as an adult, not so much.

Of course, the home was still large and lovely. Jasmine remembered the first day she arrived—sitting in the front seat of the social worker's car, the woman's cold hand patting hers on the seat—looking up at the big white house like she'd just landed on Mars. In awe.

Today, as Jasmine parked and stepped away from her car, staring up at the window of her old bedroom, she knew the day she had first arrived here was the same day her innocence had been resurrected. The same day her sad past was put to rest.

She turned and looked back down at the drive. In hindsight, she realized the day she left this house for good, was the day she'd picked that sadness right back up again.

She'd been happy at Ms. Leinie's. Those were probably the best years of her life.

It was clear now. For fifteen years she'd been sad, and she hadn't even realized it.

Turning, she stepped up onto the porch. There were the potted plants. The rocker. Some wicker chairs that were obviously newer than the ones there when she was a child. Things were clean, well taken care of. Someone must have been looking after the place for the past couple of weeks.

She spotted the porch swing.

She moved to it and sat, letting her weight drift the swing backward, and her legs dangle a bit until she moved forward again. Sighing, she let the breeze tickle through the fringe of her hair, mussing it up, while the gentle swaying of the swing unraveled her thoughts.

Ms. Leinie was making amends, even from the grave. Why she hadn't tried to do that when she was alive, Jasmine wasn't certain.

But of course, Jasmine was not available. Or ready. And Ms. Leinie likely knew that.

Jasmine knew she couldn't afford to get caught up in all the drama of this. Whatever plan Ms. Leinie had for Jack's building and the money, no matter how well intentioned, she had to steer clear. Because as much as she enjoyed seeing Jack today, and as much as her heart and body had reacted to him in ways she didn't even want to ponder, she knew it was an impossible scenario.

And it had nothing to do with Jack's parents or Ms. Leinie's hurtful words. Or that she left Jack, or that she had been pregnant.

It have everything to do with the truth. She and Jack lived in two different worlds. They wanted different things in life. And no matter how tempting or even fun it might be to try at a relationship again, it was not a good idea. In fact, it was doomed to failure from the start.

So, she had to keep all of that in mind.

She had to pull her rational, stoic self together and deal with the matters at hand in an intelligent and practical manner.

Matters of the heart were not in anyone's best interest.

Tomorrow, she would make the proper arrangements for the money. Perhaps she'd set up a fund for scholarships for high school graduates who came from her end of town. Maybe another fund for emergency food supplies for families in need. She'd find some way to invest so the money would grow and be there for a long time. That's how Ms. Leinie's money could help the kids. And she didn't have to live here to oversee that.

That's it. That's what she'd do. She'd make the arrangements with Art Manchester and be back in Atlanta before dinner tomorrow evening.

But before she left, she'd have to let Jack down easy. Of course, he was a grown man; he'd get over it. But she could see the signs—he already wanted more from her. And what he wanted, she knew she couldn't give him.

They had once been star-crossed lovers, but now they'd grown up.

She'd not start this because she couldn't finish it. She'd be damned if she'd break Jack's heart again.

JACK KNEW TODAY WAS A GIFT. AND HE WAS NOT one to look a gift horse in the mouth.

Whether this gift was a brief flicker in his life, or something to last a lifetime, he couldn't leave to chance. It was up to him. He'd decided that fact over the past few hours while sitting on his deck, his feet propped on the railing, and drinking a couple of beers while waiting for Jasmine.

The minutes rolled by in his head, from the moment he saw her standing in the bank, to the minute he watched her walk away from him down Court Street. Since then, his brain worked over every corner and angle of their conversations, and the other peripheral elements that seemed to have brought them back together again.

At least for today.

Time. He needed more time. For all he knew, she planned to go back to Atlanta tomorrow after her meeting. He had to get her to stay longer.

On the other hand, there had to be *reason* for her to come back.

He wanted that reason to be him. Nothing else.

Not for the kids. The project. Her inheritance. Ms. Leinie.

For him.

God, he still loved her. After all these years, nothing was different. Her mind, her face, her eyes, her heart... Her soul captured him years ago, and today, he was caught up in the mere essence of her even more.

He couldn't screw things up, and he wouldn't. As much emotion as he'd been through today, she'd been through more. There were too many years between them that needed to be crossed. A lot of hurt and pain to cross over. Today they'd shared only a few hours' time, a mere dent in an attempt to get back what they once had. It was a start.

But it almost seemed too much to tackle.

"Hi. I let myself in. I hope that was okay."

Slowly, Jack pulled his heels off the railing and tugged his brain back to reality. He placed his boots on the deck and stood to face Jasmine.

It was more than okay. She was home.

Chapter Eight

At first, Jasmine thought Jack was angry. He just stood there staring at her. Then his face broke into a grin, and even though she fought it, her heart melted a little.

"Of course it's okay, Jasmine. I left the door unlocked for you. Had dinner?"

"Oh. No." She hadn't even thought about food. "But I'm really not hungry."

Jack glanced at his watch. "It's nearly eight o'clock. You barely picked at your salad at lunch. Can I at least get that for you?"

She probably should eat, but... "Thanks, Jack. I'm fine. More than anything, I would like to head to bed early. I'm a little tired. Would you mind?"

"Of course not." He crossed the deck toward her. "Let's get you settled."

Jasmine followed him into the great room. She'd left a couple of packages and her purse on the table. "I'll just grab these."

He turned. "Did you find what you needed in town?"

"I did."

Small talk. Maybe they were both tired.

Maybe that was a good thing.

"I really appreciate your hospitality, Jack," she added.

His gaze didn't falter. "Hospitality? Jasmine..." His words trailed off. "Come on, we don't have to be so formal. Look, I—"

She cut him off, uncertain where he was heading, or why she'd even said what she said. Weary confusion was setting in. "Sorry." She placed a hand on his forearm. "I know that sounded stilted. My brain is just spent. I think I'm talked out, and thought out, for the day."

He placed his hand on top of hers. "Same here. It's been a long day. C'mon."

Their hands dropped, and Jack moved through the room toward the staircase. She followed him up to the second level and then across the second-story landing, which was actually a balcony over the great room. The rich wood logs of the walls looked to be cedar, and as she glanced down at Jack's comfortable home below, a pang deep as Falls Lake landed with an ugly plop in her gut.

Jack's home.

All these years she'd wondered about him. Where he was, how he was living, with whom... And he'd never left this spot. He was here all along. Just where she'd left him.

"My room is down the hall." He thumbed toward a door at the end of the landing and then twisted the doorknob to the room in front of them. "This one is yours." He stepped out of the way and shoved his hands into his pockets. She wondered if the gesture was to avoid touching her, and if she projected that *hands off* attitude. He nodded toward the room; Jasmine followed his gaze and stepped inside.

The room was lovely. *More* than lovely. It was awesome.

An antique cherry sleigh bed sat in the center; a log cabin quilt draped over the mattress. Matching nightstands bookended both sides, and a tall, antique highboy dresser stood to her right. The walls were the same rich cedar logs, and the curtains to two immense windows were pulled back, revealing a dusky view of Falls Mountain and the Blue Ridge Mountains beyond.

Her breath caught. "Wow, Jack. That is some view."

He stood directly behind her, she knew, because she heard his intake of breath, and felt the warmth of his exhale on the back of her neck. "Best view in the house," he said. "And the sunrise is guaranteed to wake you in the morning if you don't pull those curtains."

She shook her head. "Naw. I want to wake up with the heat of the sun on my cheeks."

"I'd rather you wake up with the heat of my kisses on your cheeks."

Jasmine turned. "Jack!"

He caught her up in his arms. "Jasmine, don't talk."

"Why?"

"Because you are all talked out. Me too."

She shook her head. "I don't understand."

"Sh..."

Jack cupped her face in his hands, drew her closer and touched her lips with his. He leaned in closer, the pressure of his mouth increasing over hers—warm, firm, soft. Heaven.

A sensation Jasmine had not felt in years zinged up from her tummy to her chest, and she crowded closer. A piece of her heart, missing for years, locked back into place. Her packages landed on the floor with a thud and a rattle, and her arms went about his neck.

Jack's fingers threaded through her hair, and his lips parted slightly. Jasmine teased back with hers and, daringly, with the tip of her tongue. Jack groaned and walked her backward toward the wall, trapping her between him and the cedar logs.

That action was nearly her undoing. His lips caressed hers, his heated breath played over her mouth, the length of his body fit snug against hers. Her hands traveled down to his shoulders, biceps...

He broke the kiss with a sigh. "Oh, hell, Jazzy..."

Pulling back, Jack's gaze played over her face. He swept the hair back over her forehead and trailed his fingertips over her cheek and down to her chin.

Jasmine bit her lip and glanced at his mouth. "Kiss me again," she whispered. It was the last thing she needed.

Jack pressed against her in response. That action sent another curl of desire racing through her body. "Jasmine," he said softly. "I don't want to mess this up."

Her chest lifted and fell. "What do you mean?"

"I'm still in love with you, Jazzy. I've never stopped. I knew it the moment I saw you in the bank. But I don't want to do anything tonight that is going to confuse things."

"Meaning you want to kiss me."

"I want to kiss you and more, but I want you to be sure. And I don't think—"

She stopped him with a forefinger on his lips. Jack's eyes closed at the touch, and Jasmine relished the feel of his firm, moist lips beneath her fingertip. "Jack, just kiss me once more, and then tell me good night."

"What?"

"You heard me."

His eyes flickered open, and Jasmine let her finger drag off his mouth. Jack pressed her back into the wall and angled his mouth over hers.

He tasted her, holding her face still, raking his mouth over hers. Jasmine breathed deep of his scent, inhaling his kisses over her lips, and moving in sync with his rhythm. She combed through all of her emotions, sensations, imprinting the moment in her brain. On her heart. She didn't know if this would ever happen again, this kiss, this closeness, and if it didn't, she wanted to remember the feel of everything she was experiencing. Forever.

She grasped him at the waist; her fingers splayed over his ribs. It took everything in her not to snake her hands to his chest and rip his shirt free from his body.

But she didn't.

Jack's kisses slowed, and so did her breathing. Finally, with one last nibble, he pulled back, peering deep into Jasmine's eyes.

After a moment, he stepped back, pushing away from the wall. And from her. His gaze lingered for another small moment, and then he whispered, "Good night, Jazzy. See you in the morning."

Then he left. The room was suddenly cold and impartial. And she had to remind herself that being alone was what she wanted. Right?

JASMINE, 1999

Section by section, I watched the lights on the football field blink off, darkness filling the void between the school and the bleachers. Standing next to Jack's truck, I suddenly felt alone in the dark and a little frightened, but I kept my eyes glued to the light over the door at the back of the school where I knew Jack would soon be exiting.

Coach Blanton had asked him to hang back after the game and team meeting, because he'd wanted to talk to him about something. Jack didn't know what, and I was a little worried.

I waited because we were going for late pizza at Mario's.

Usually the football crowd gathered there after the game. This would be the third Friday night date with Jack, and I was looking forward to it.

I sighed, trying to rid myself of my nerves, anticipating him walking out that door. Whenever I thought of Jack, I felt giddy inside. Just looking at him made me breathless. Sitting next to him in his truck made me almost dizzy with pleasure. I was falling for him, hard. And I think he was for me, too.

I could only dare to hope.

The back door burst open, and I jerked upright, watching. Three of the players left the building, punching each other and walking off toward their trucks, a little to my left. I recognized them but didn't know them personally. One was Andrew Pointer. Everyone knew Andrew. Class jokester and quarterback.

They stopped up short, and Andrew looked my way. I glanced away, trying to appear disinterested. I heard them talking, low and under their breath. Then Andrew shouted.

"Hey! What are you doing over there, honey?"

I didn't answer, just kept looking toward the door, praying for Jack to come out any second.

But they sauntered closer, and as they did, my chest lifted and fell with the upkick of my heartbeat. When they stopped right in front of me, I turned my stare their way.

"If you are looking for Jack, he'll be out in a minute," I said, wanting them to realize that I wasn't here alone. Not for long, anyway.

Andrew stepped closer. He angled his face, staring into my eyes. "So, you're with Jack, huh?" He chuckled and looked at his friends, right and left. "Not for long from what I hear."

My face must have screwed up because he laughed at my expression. What did he mean?

I said nothing.

He continued to taunt. "So, I always wondered what it would be like to have a piece of a girl like you. You want to show me, sweetheart?" He crowded closer, and I dropped my purse, putting my hands up on his chest and pushing. *Where is Jack?*

"What are you doing?" I shouted.

"I can hold her, Andy, if you want."

Panic tore through me. "Get away! Help!" I clawed at his face.

He grabbed me by the shoulders and shoved me back against the truck. Pain rattled my spine. His mouth smeared across mine while I whipped my head back and forth in protest. His hot hand fumbled for my breast. His pelvis crushed into mine.

I whimpered and tried to fight him. Another set of hands grabbed mine and jammed me back against the truck. I tried to make as much noise as I could, squealing and kicking backward, trying to pound my foot into the sidewall—but his mouth and body stifled my feeble attempts.

The other two crowded closer, as if they were shielding Andrew. I knew the parking lot was dark and barely anyone was around. I prayed Jack would come out soon.

Andrew burst back. "Damn, I'm hard," he said. "Get ready, bitch. This ain't gonna be like Jack." Then he added. "Hold her against the truck. Eric, watch that damn door."

This ain't gonna be like Jack. All I could think about was that Jack would never want me after this. Jack and I had never... I had never....

I kicked and screamed. A hand went over my mouth. I watched Andrew jerk down his zipper and his sweaty hand went under my dress. Groping.

Oh, God, no...

Inside, I was frantic. My mind blurry. Everything was fast

and slow, all at the same time. Didn't know what to do. Couldn't do anything.

Hands were pinned. Body numb. Couldn't scream any longer....

I prayed. Please, God. Let Jack—

"Hey! *Hey!*"

"Goddamn. Coach!" One of them yelled.

My hands fell limp against my body, released. Andrew pushed back, and my skirt fell in front. He gave me an intense look and zipped up his jeans. "Later," he said.

Then he was gone because out of nowhere, Jack sailed into him and tackled him to the asphalt. I screamed as they rolled and then Jack was on top, pummeling the hell out of Andrew's face. In seconds, two men jerked him up and away from Andrew. Coach Blanton and someone else. He pulled Jack back and held him, while Jack looked at me and flailed his arms, yelling.

"Let me go! Jasmine!"

Couch yanked him. "Hold on there, Jack. Dammit."

Jack stilled but his expression was frantic. I felt cold and confused, like I was standing on the periphery. Outside looking in.

Coach kicked at Andrew. "Get up and get out of here, goddamn it. Go!"

Jack wailed and shrugged out of Coach's grasp. "You goddamn sonofabitch!" He yelled at Andrew and darted forward, but then whirled back and raced toward me instead. His hands cupped my face, and he brushed the hair out of my eyes. He stared at me, his chest heaving. "Are you all right? Goddammit, Jazzy," he said, breathless, "Are you all right?"

I could hear the other trucks leaving the parking lot and silently breathed a sigh of relief.

I nodded. "Y-yes. I'm. Okay." I was shaking like hell.

Coach Blanton stepped up and looked at Jack. "See what I mean? Think about what I told you. For everyone's sake."

Jack stared back and gathered me closer, protecting me from what I suddenly realized was more than Andrew. Breathing hard, he held the coach's stare for a few more minutes and then turned to me. "Let's go."

He sheltered me as he unlocked the truck and helped me inside from the driver's side. He followed. Doors locked, he started the truck, revved the engine, and peeled out of the high school parking lot, staring at the coach until he was out of sight.

JASMINE SAT UP, PANTING. SHE FLUNG THE COVERS back and let her legs hang over the side of the high bed, exhaling deeply, as if she'd been holding a massive breath for years. Slowly, the air eased out of her lungs, and her shoulders stopped shaking.

Propping her elbows on her knees, she rubbed the heels of her hands over her eyes. Finally, she took another deep breath and looked across the room and out the window. A full moon sat over the mountain, spilling light into the room.

She supposed it was normal that she would dream about Jack. About Harbor Falls. About Ms. Leinie. But she hadn't thought about the attack in the high school parking lot for years, and she wasn't sure why she would dream about it now.

Much like every other bad life experience, she'd pushed that scene to the far recesses of her brain and out of her heart. Less painful that way, of course. Safer. But ever since she'd stepped out of her car in Harbor Falls this morning, memories long repressed came zinging back, playing out in her head, her mind, and now her dreams.

Perhaps that's why you can't go home again, Jasmine.

Things forgotten still lie in wait, poised and ready to inflict unwelcome memories upon your return.

She slipped off the bed and padded to the adjoining bathroom. Jasmine turned on the light and splashed cold water onto her face and then dried off with a towel. Looking up, she studied herself in the mirror.

Bare. Exposed. No makeup. Hair mussed. Wearing only Jack's T-shirt and a pair of panties she'd picked up earlier while strolling around some shops on Main Street in town.

Stripped bare, she was herself. And deep down, what did that really mean?

What was left?

What does one really have when everything else is gone?

She pondered that, watching the rise and fall of her chest in the reflection. Her heart was still beating fast from the dream. The memory.

Jack had shielded her, protected her, and later when they were far away from the school, and those awful boys, and the coaches—when they were safely parked back on the farm in their spot—

This spot—

He'd held her all night. He didn't touch her inappropriately. He didn't ask anything of her. He cherished her and told her he loved her. He made her feel safe and secure and wanted.

Safe.

I am still in love with you, Jazzy. I've never stopped.

Then a few weeks later, she gave herself to him fully. He protested, and said no, for a long time. But she had wanted him so badly, and then once they did....

Jasmine looked long at her reflection, then turned and left the room.

THE BED SQUEAKED AND JACK ROLLED OVER, HIS eyes adjusting to the dark.

"Jasmine?"

"Jack."

He sat up quickly. "What are you doing?"

"Tell me what the coach meant."

"What?"

He rubbed his eyes and shook his head. He hadn't been kidding earlier when he said he'd sleep better tonight than he had in fifteen years—he'd been sound asleep until just this moment. "I don't understand."

She moved on her knees, closer. She looked like an angel, backlit by the moonlight coming in the window. Wisps of short hair, golden at the edges, framed her face.

"Tell me what he meant. That night. Remember? That night in the parking lot after the game. That boy, Andrew...."

At once, Jack's gut tightened. "Sonofabitch. Glad that asshole left for college and never came back to Harbor Falls."

She huffed out a breath. "It's okay. And yes, he was an asshole. But I need to know what the coach said that night. What he meant. He said something like—"

"Think about what I told you." Dammit. *Why bring this up now?*

"Yes. What did he mean?"

Jack fell back against the pillow and reached for Jasmine. "Come here. Please."

Sighing, she did. Jasmine fell into his arms, her head in the crook of his chest and shoulder. "It was about me, wasn't it?"

He waited a minute and said, "Yes. He told me not to date you."

"Why? Oh."

He fiddled with a strand of her hair. "Hell, Jazzy. Coach thought he owned all of us. He didn't want any of us to date, period. Didn't want us distracted. But he was on me a lot for dating you."

"Because my mother was black."

"Probably. Yes."

"You were a star player."

"Yep."

"You could have gone pro." Her voice was soft, wispy. Tired.

"Maybe, if I'd finished college, Jazzy, but I didn't. And anyway..."

"You quit the team."

Jack turned and faced Jasmine. "Why are we talking about this, Jasmine? I mean, as much as I am loving having you in my bed, I hadn't expected that when you were here, we'd be talking about my football career, or lack thereof."

"You quit for me. Because of me."

"I quit because I love you, and I'll be damned if anyone was going to make me do something I didn't want to do—like give you up."

Her eyes misted over. He watched the even rise and fall of her breasts.

"That night... You protected me. You were like an angry lion protecting what was yours. You took care of me, held me, made me feel so safe. Safer than I had ever felt in my life."

Jack ran his fingertips down Jasmine's cheek. "I'd do it again a thousand times over. Then. Today. Whenever."

"You still love me."

His heart swelled. Hooking a finger under her chin, he lifted her head until her eyes met his. "I never stopped, Jasmine."

He caught the tears spilling over her bottom eyelid and swiped them away with a forefinger. She tilted her head and ever so gently kissed his lips. Softly.

"Jack?" she whispered.

"Yes?"

"Make me feel safe. Hold me again tonight, all night long. Just like you did that night all those years ago. Would you?"

Jack pulled her closer and exhaled. Her head rested on his chest. His heart absorbed her presence. "There is nothing more in the world I could ever want."

Chapter Nine

Jasmine woke, blinking at the sunlight streaming through Jack's bedroom windows.

Jack's bedroom. She blinked again and rolled over. Jack was gone.

Since it was daylight, she assumed he was up and getting ready for work, something she should do herself. Not get ready for work, of course, but get ready for her meeting with Art Manchester at ten o'clock.

But she didn't move, staring at Jack's pillow. Reaching out, she ran her fingertips over the indentation where his head had been. She swore the pillow was still warm. Maybe he'd not been up long.

Leaning in, Jasmine put her nose next to the pillow and breathed deep. She inhaled Jack's scent and a calmness came over her. Calm. He'd always made her feel that way. Safe and peaceful.

She should get up, but the quiet was nice. Her brain wandered a little over the past day's events, her conviction to let Jack down easily, the heartfelt goodnight kiss they'd shared before bed, the hours of sleeping in his arms.

Her heart was conflicted.

No. Her brain was conflicted. Her heart knew....

Not thinking about that.

Sleeping with him was wrong. She couldn't break his heart again. She'd already decided she was telling him today that they could never make this work. Why did she succumb to the safe and warm confines of his kisses, his arms, and his bed?

She sat up, took a sniff, and stretched. Coffee. He must be downstairs.

Sleeping in Jack's arms was wonderful, but it was over. They'd both had a good night's sleep, and that was that.

Now, it was time to get down to business.

She glanced at the digital clock beside Jack's bed. Not yet seven. Plenty of time for a shower and a little research on her laptop before the meeting. When she met with Art and the bank officials this morning, she wanted her ducks in a row.

An hour later, Jasmine gathered her things and headed downstairs to the great room. The coffee was still on, hot and waiting, a large mug sitting in front of the carafe. A platter of cinnamon rolls sat on the counter. And sitting beside that was a tented piece of paper with her name on the outside.

She picked it up and slowly opened the note. The message was simple.

Help yourself to coffee and a roll.

Can't wait to see you later.

I love you. Jack

Later. He was expecting to see her later. This day was not going to be easy.

"THIS SHOULDN'T BE SO COMPLICATED."

Jasmine looked up from the papers, books and files spread across Carl Robbin's desk. She, Carl, and Art Manchester had discussed the funds in the safe deposit box for the past thirty minutes, trying to come to some logical conclusions about how Jasmine could best make use of Ms. Leinie's money. "And it shouldn't be. What's going on here?"

The thing was, there appeared to be some loopholes that Art hadn't discovered or expected, and wasn't privy to until sometime late yesterday afternoon.

Jasmine looked at Art. "I don't understand. Yesterday you said the will read that Ms. Leinie was simply leaving me the contents of her safe deposit box. And you said that was it." She faced Carl. "And Mr. Robbins, you mentioned that the contents of the boxes are generally unknown to the bank, so there was no way you knew what Ms. Leinie had in there. Correct?"

Carl nodded. "Yes, but now that we know, there are some legal ramifications, such as inheritance taxes, etc."

"I understand that, and it's expected. But I don't feel like I'm getting the entire story here."

Carl glanced at Art, who stared back at him. Then they both looked at Jasmine. Finally, Art pushed his chair back and stood. "There have been some recent developments. Some... stipulations. Stipulations we wish we could work around but can't, and we're not sure that you will agree to them. So, depending on the decisions you make soon, this could get very complicated, or it could be very simple. I don't know the answers, and frankly, you are probably going to want to think about it."

"Great." Stipulations. Ones she had not anticipated. What the hell was he talking about? Ridiculous stipulations that made no sense, likely. This day was not going as planned.

"Look," she began. "Let's just make this as simple as possible. I've done the research, and I know a fair amount about wills and trusts. I'll establish a trust for the funds and put the money into an account in Atlanta so I can easily monitor."

She looked at Mr. Robbins. "I'm sure you can assist me with that transfer. The money will be held for scholarships for qualifying graduate seniors. I'll draw up the guidelines, and we'll get all the legalities firmed up over the next few weeks. I'll oversee everything from Atlanta. I don't see an issue."

Art shook his head. "It won't work, Jasmine."

"Sure, it will."

"No. Not according to this," Art told her, pointing to a paper on the desk. "The money has to stay in the community."

"That's fine," Jasmine replied. "It can stay right here in Harbor Falls." She glanced at Carl. "Scratch that comment about the transfer. We'll establish a bank account here. That's probably better, anyway. I can still oversee everything from Atlanta."

Art cleared his throat. "I'm afraid that won't work either."

"Why?"

"Because the trustee over the money has to be a Harbor Falls resident."

Jasmine rolled her eyes. "Either you or the bank can hold the trust, Art. That's fine."

"We can definitely do that for you, but there is more."

"More?" *What now?*

Art exhaled. "Before you can decide about or make provisions for the money, you must commit to living in Harbor Falls for at least a year."

"What? That's ridiculous."

"It's right here." He held out the paper he'd been pointing at. "It's legal. It didn't surface until late yesterday afternoon after Ms. Leinie's cousin found it in her desk. This is her last will and testament, written, witnessed, and notarized a few days before her death. It clearly states that it revokes all previous wills and codicils. And yes, she was definitely of sound mind when she wrote it."

She took a deep breath. "But what about Ms. Leinie's letter to me? The one she left in the box? Her indications were pretty darned clear there that it was up to me how to disperse the funds."

"And that letter was dated when?"

She couldn't remember. "Hold on." She reached into her briefcase and pulled out the envelope. Carefully, she removed the letter and unfolded it. "The second day of January, this year."

"The same date as the will filed with me." Art pushed an alternative paper toward her. "The date on this last will and testament found late yesterday, is just two weeks ago."

Jasmine took it and slowly sat back in her seat. There, she read Ms. Leinie's last words. The letter was brief, just one page, and, surprisingly, it all had to do with the money she had left to her. It read:

REGARDING THE FUNDS OF MY SAFE DEPOSIT BOX. *Those funds, as stated in the letter in the box, continue to go to Ms. Jasmine Walker. However, I am now placing two restrictions on that money that I would like Ms. Walker to carry out. Those requests are: 1) the money will go to support a community building and food bank currently being built on Court Street. These funds do not go toward the building itself, but for the daily operational expenses for family support services—management, staff, food, supplies, and so on; and 2) the family support services are to be operated by someone who has lived in the community and knows the community, and for at least the first year, that would be Ms. Jasmine Walker. She will coordinate services with the owner of the building, who is Mr. Jack Ackerman.*

. . .

FURTHERMORE, MS. WALKER MUST LIVE IN HARBOR Falls for a minimum of one year in order to proceed with these plans. She has lived in Atlanta for many years, and I want her to remember what small-town living is like before she takes full control of this project. If she cannot agree to this provision, or if after one year she does not want to move forward, she forfeits all assets bequeathed to her to Mr. Jack Ackerman, who will proceed with my wishes.

JASMINE LAID THE PAPER IN HER LAP AND LOOKED AT the two men. "So, I either have to move to Harbor Falls or give up the estate entirely to Jack?"

Art nodded. "That's about the gist of it."

Jasmine glanced toward the window, watching the lazy town of Harbor Falls drift by. Return to Harbor Falls? *Oh, Ms. Leinie. What have you done?*

JACK LOOKED ACROSS THE DESK AT CAM PARKER. "You're kidding me. I own the building?"

"Yes, as soon as all the legalities are taken care of."

"I don't understand. You said last week Ms. Leinie had made provisions for the completion of the project through a trust, and I would work with someone here at the bank to get all the details worked out. Then once the construction was finished, my obligation was done."

"Yes, that was right. Then. But now—"

"Now what?"

"Now there is a recent development. The building and land have been left to you. It's all right here."

Jack looked at a sheet of paper in Cam's hands. "What is that?"

"Ms. Leinie's last will and testament. Her cousin found it on her desk and delivered it to Art Machester, who is handling her estate, yesterday afternoon. It precedes all other paperwork. Perhaps you should read it."

Cam handed him a piece of paper. He noticed in was page two of the document. "Where is page one?" he asked.

Cam nodded toward the door. "With Carl Robbins. There are some details there he needs to discuss with another client."

"Oh." Jack settled back to look at Ms. Leinie's last words:

REGARDING THE BUILDING UNDER CONSTRUCTION *on Court Street, I bequeath the land and the completed structure to Mr. Jack Ackerman. The necessary funds for the completion of the construction project are in trust at Harbor Falls Bank & Trust, under the management of Mr. Cam Parker and Mr. Carl Robbins. Mr. Ackerman will work with the bank to complete the project. Furthermore, I am placing two restrictions on the ownership of the property: 1) Mr. Ackerman must utilize the building as a community building and food pantry, to support the local residents. The building may not be used for any other purpose than to support the families of the local community; and 2) even though he will own the building, the family services offered within the building will be managed by a Harbor Falls resident, Ms. Jasmine Walker, who must commit to living in Harbor Falls for at least one year in order to oversee the family services efforts.*

IN THAT REGARD, IF MS. WALKER DOES NOT COMPLY *with the stipulations indicated in this document, that is, to live in Harbor Falls for one year, she will turn over her portion of the estate to Mr. Ackerman, who will proceed with my wishes. If*

Mr. Ackerman cannot, or chooses not, to fulfill the stipulations of the building and its management, then the land and the building, and as well as the assets bequeathed to Ms. Walker, will be turned over to the state of North Carolina to do with as they wish.

JACK BLEW OUT A BREATH. "SHIT." HE STOOD THEN and raked a hand through his hair, still staring at the page.

"Excuse me?"

"Cam, this is not good. Not good at all. Does Jasmine know?"

"I believe they are meeting right now. Should we see if we can meet with them?"

Jack paced. "I don't know. I'm just not sure how this is going to sit with her. I need to think."

Cam agreed. "I'm more worried about you. If she foregoes all the assets, then it all falls on you to manage the community building, staff, and everything else."

"Or it goes back to the state."

"Right. But there are people here in Harbor Falls who could benefit."

"Yes. That is definitely true."

Jack looked at Cam. "I don't have time for this. As much as I loved Ms. Leinie and her vision for helping families, this is all out of my comfort level. I dig in the dirt, plant trees, and mow lawns. Hell, even acting as contractor for that building of hers was a stretch for me, but I did it because she trusted me. I do not know how to run a community building."

Cam shrugged. "Maybe you won't have to know. Maybe Ms. Walker will stay in Harbor Falls, and it won't be your problem. All you need to do is manage the property."

Not my problem. Right.

Jack just stared at him. What he did not want was for

Jasmine to feel forced to stay in Harbor Falls. This didn't bode well for either of them. All of this was too new and too complicated to wrap their brains around. Their relationship notwithstanding.

"You don't understand. Either way, it's a problem. In more ways than you know."

Jasmine didn't need to be handed a reason to bolt. Why would Ms. Leinie tie up this land and funds with these stipulations? What was she after?

To get you two back together.

Jasmine was right. Her plan was more than helping families at risk. Her plan was getting them back together.

A knock sounded at the door, and before Cam could answer, Carl Robbins, Art Manchester, and Jasmine walked through the opened door. Her gaze landed on him. He could clearly read her expression.

Lawyer face. His worse fears suddenly materialized.

"Jack, we need to talk," she said.

He nodded. "Yes, we do."

Chapter Ten

J ack stepped forward and lightly grasped her elbow. Jasmine reminded herself not to react to that touch, although her heart pitter-pattered a bit.

"Gentleman," he said, "if you'll excuse us, I think Ms. Walker and I would like to discuss some things in private."

"Jack?" She gazed into his eyes, questioning.

He stared back and said, "Perhaps we can take a walk or...."

Cam interrupted. "Use my office. We'll let you discuss and just give us a shout when you're ready."

The men left, and Jasmine wondered just how the next few minutes were going to pan out. The door closed.

"Let's sit over here." Jack pulled a chair away from the table and turned it slightly.

Jasmine moved forward. "I really think I prefer to stand." *I think, anyway. If my knees will hold me up.* Then she blurted. "Don't worry, Jack. We can find a way out of this. We don't have to do what she says."

Jack stood silent for a moment. "Or we could."

"Could what?"

"Do what she said. Fulfill her wishes."

Jasmine laughed, hoping she didn't sound nervous. Hoping her poker face was holding up. She sighed and then sat. *Better.* "Jack, let's be realistic."

She wanted to be firm, direct. To the point. Reasonable.

But something was wrong. With her. She felt unbalanced, which was unusual. Things like this rarely threw her for a loop.

Of course, when she dealt with things like this in her professional life, they were not personal. Like now.

"Jasmine, I am being realistic. Just hear me out." He pulled up a chair and sat across from her.

This wasn't going the way she wanted. Of course, neither yesterday nor today was going as expected. "All right. I'm listening."

He took a deep breath and let it out. Slowly. "First, remember that anything is possible, and we just need to—"

She fidgeted in her seat. "Jack, look," she interrupted. *Dammit. No use stringing this out.* "Some things are not possible. I just need to be honest here. I want to do good for Ms. Leinie. She saved a lot of money, and I really want the kids and families of Harbor Falls who need it to benefit—but I'm not the person to make this thing happen. I can't. I have other obligations."

"So do I, Jasmine. That's why I think that the two of us together can make this work. Let's just try to figure out the details of how we can make this happen for those kids."

That's all she'd been able to think about. Well, partly. "Jack, I get it. I want to help the kids here. Truly, I do, but I can't live in Harbor Falls."

"What?"

"I can't live here."

He sat back. "Ever?"

She blew out a breath. "I... I don't think so, Jack. I'm not cut out for small-town living any longer. And Harbor Falls is just not that friendly to me."

"You're letting the past creep into the present, Jazzy. Don't."

She huffed. "Not that easy, Jack. There is a lot of history here. A lot that even you don't know about."

He stared at her for a moment. "So, tell me."

She shook her head. "No. There is no use. I'm not comfortable here any longer, and I can't live my life in a place where I am not welcome. So...."

"So that's it? You're not cut out for small-town living, so you just give up on the kids, and Ms. Leinie's dream, and... And me?"

At that moment, she felt like she must own the hardest, coldest heart south of the Mason-Dixon. "Wait. You're jumping to conclusions. And I'm ahead of myself."

"Then just get to it, Jasmine. What is it you want to say?"

"Take the money, Jack. I can give it to you. You can make this work. You'll find a way. I'm giving the money over to you."

He stood and the chair screeched on the hardwood floor. "I don't want the damn money, Jasmine. I want you. Don't you get that?"

"Then why are you talking circles about the kids and the money and doing good things to honor Ms. Leinie? Then why don't you just come right out and say what you want?" Her voice had raised, and during those words, she stood and was facing Jack. He stared back at her with eyes full of conflict. Of love, hurt, confusion....

"I want you, Jazzy," he said, his voice soft. "I want you by my side. I want you in my house and in my bed every single damn night. I love you. I have always loved you. And now that I've seen you again, touched you, kissed you... Well, I can't bear to think about living the rest of my life without you." He

89

closed his eyes, his head shaking, and Jasmine watched the anguish wash over his face. "I'm not above begging you to stay... But it's apparent you don't feel the same way."

Jasmine knew what she said next would be the defining moment in their relationship. She had to measure her words carefully and make the right decision about what she truly wanted.

"Jack," she whispered, her voice as calm as she could make it. "You are firmly embedded in this community. You and your family. You have a beautiful home that needs a woman in it, and children. You need both in your life. I know this. It's what you've wanted, sought, since we were kids. You love me. I know this too. And I'm looking at you right now and telling you, with all of my heart, that I love you back. I always have, and I always will. But I'm not the woman to give you those babies. I'm not the woman to sleep in your bed. I can't. I *can't* give you babies. I can't live here. And I can't love you like you want me to love you."

Her eyes stung. "Jack, take the money so it won't go back to the state. Build the building and find someone to manage it. There are a lot of good people here in Harbor Falls. I'm going back to Atlanta and doing the work that I do with children there. My place is not here. It was never here. I can never overcome the heartache of being the poor little mixed girl who came from the wrong side of the tracks.

"So, I'm leaving. Don't say anything. Please. Just let me walk out of here with some dignity. I'll get with Art on my way out and tell him my decision."

She turned her back on Jack then, opened the office door, and stepped out of his life.

Chapter Eleven

A t ten minutes after eight, Jasmine entered her front door, locked it behind her, and dropped briefcase, purse and mail on the entryway sideboard. Simultaneously, she kicked off her heels and began stripping off her clothing. First peeling off her suit jacket and skirt, then blouse, bra, underwear and hose, letting one article after another drip to the floor, on the trek toward her bedroom and master bath.

But first, she stopped in her kitchen, standing naked as a jaybird in the middle of it, uncorked a bottle and poured herself a glass of Merlot.

"Now, bubbles."

For the next ten minutes, she took pains to turn her bathroom into a spa. Water just the right temperature, bubbles, low lights, candles, and music. A rolled towel sat waiting for her head, and with the glass of wine on the table beside her whirlpool tub, she slipped into the silky-softness, eased her body into the water up to her neck, laid back and closed her eyes.

This was a long time coming.

Two long, miserable days' worth.

After returning to Atlanta on Wednesday afternoon, she had plunged herself into work, every single minute of the day Thursday and Friday. Up early, she hit the gym at her condo complex before six, working out perhaps longer and more diligently than usual. Later, showered and dressed, she was out the door by seven-thirty, navigating Atlanta rush hour traffic, and in her office by eight-fifteen. She worked late both nights to make up for the time she spent in Harbor Falls.

The days were an endless series of meetings with families, therapists, social workers, and mediators, interspersed with a couple of hearings, a dentist appointment, and working on a couple of heartbreaking cases.

Cases she feared she was going to lose. Children reinstated with families that worried her; parents making commitments she knew could not carry through. The bottom line being that children might suffer.

It was the one thing she continually vowed she would fight for—that children didn't suffer. That they had safe, secure environments to grow up in. That they had healthy, adequate food to eat. A warm bed to sleep in.

But they would. Suffer.

She'd seen it way too often. There were days she wondered why she tried so hard.

The system routinely had other ideas what was best for kids. Ideas that did not meet her expectations. Promises made were too easily broken.

There were times the system sucked royally.

She rolled her shoulders a little in the water to grind out the kinks, certain the wine, hot water, and bubbles would not do their trick. She was wound tight, and it wasn't only because of work.

Jack.

Jack's face wouldn't leave her alone. Her time in Harbor Falls wouldn't let her be. Smells and voices and sights and conversations came drifting back without notice. And she kept thinking about the building on Court Street, down the street from the house she grew up in. The money. What would happen now? And for some reason, she kept thinking about her father. Where he was and why he had never tried to contact her. She thought about Ms. Leinie and her wishes.

And that she was, once again, letting her down.

Of course, there was Jack, whose heart she had broken. Again.

And then here she was. Alone. In Atlanta. Running away from it all.

Again.

Her cell phone rattled on the small table beside her tub. She'd purposely turned down the sound because she didn't want to be bothered this evening. But something made her tip it up and look at the caller info on the screen.

Ben Samuels. A local cop who sometimes worked domestic cases.

She closed her eyes, pushed the button, and put the phone to her ear. "Yes?"

Ben's voice was soft and slow on the other end. "Jasmine, sorry to bother you on a Friday night, but I just wanted you to know in case you caught the evening news."

She exhaled. This would not be good. "Okay. Who is it?"

He cleared his throat. "The Shepherd case you worked where the kids went back to the mom a few weeks ago. Remember?"

She sat up, water sloshing. Of course, she remembered. Timmy Shepherd. Four-year-old abused by the mom's boyfriend. The jerk been sent up to prison. The child took months to recover in foster care. He and his brother had been reinstated to the mother's care after she spent time in counseling and parenting classes. Jasmine had fought the reinstatement, convinced that the mom wasn't ready, hadn't fully rehabilitated, and that she'd repeat the same bad news boyfriend behavior.

Social services thought differently.

"Yes. What happened?"

Ben took a breath. "Tim was shot tonight. Didn't make it." He paused a second. "The new boyfriend had a gun. The six-year-old found it. And well...."

Stunned, she said nothing for a moment. "Okay, Ben. I get it. Thanks for giving me a heads up."

"You okay?"

She didn't say anything else. Couldn't.

"Jasmine?"

"Yeah, yeah. I'm okay. Thanks."

She ended the call and placed the phone back on the table. Slowly, she slipped back into the water, sinking in over her head.

***

ON SATURDAY, JACK LIFTED THE POST-HOLE DIGGER and jammed it into the ground. He jimmied the thing, spread the handles apart, squeezed them together again, and lifted out a large clod of dirt, tossing it to the side. He repeated the process several more times until the hole he was digging was deep enough and wide enough to plant the shrub he needed to plant behind Suzie Matthews' deck. And until the sweat was rolling down his neck and down his back.

"Goodness, Jack. Slow down there a minute."

Glancing up, he watched Suzie move down the back steps, a glass of iced tea in her hand that was sweating almost as much as he was. "If you aren't a sight for sore eyes."

"Me?" Suzie asked.

"No, the tea."

Suzie chuckled and handed him the glass. He didn't wait

to take a long drink of the cold and sweet liquid. "Ah. Suzie Matthews, you sure know how to please a man."

She laughed. "Well, if that's all it takes, then I've been doing it wrong." She winked and sat on the step. "Why don't you sit a minute, Jack? You've been wrestling that hole for over an hour now."

Suzie and his older brother Sam were in the same class at Harbor Falls High. They'd all been good friends ever since. He and Sam had taken care of Suzie's landscaping at the inn for years.

"I need to get this done."

"Hot date tonight?"

He huffed. "No. No hot date. Just a lot to check off the list today."

"Keeping your hands and mind busy, huh?"

He cocked his head. "Why do you say that?"

She shrugged. "Heard down at Ralph's that you and Nora broke up."

Nora. That seemed ages ago. When was that? Just last weekend? "Yeah. We did. But that's old news."

"Then why the hell are you taking it out on that poor hole in my yard? Mercy, Jack, you could bury someone in it. All I wanted was an azalea!"

He looked back at the hole. Hell. He had gotten a little carried away, but the physical exertion felt good. And yes, by God, it had taken his mind off things. "Jasmine was in town this week," he said, not looking at Suzie.

"Jasmine Walker?"

He glanced back. "Yeah."

"I haven't seen her in years. How is she?"

Jack exhaled. "I guess she's fine. She left rather abruptly."

"Was that who you called me about needing a room?"

He nodded. "It was."

"Where'd she end up staying?"

Jack stared at her. "With me."

"Ah."

"We didn't do anything."

"Jack, you're an adult. So is Jasmine. You're not kids any longer."

He glanced off. Suddenly, his head hurt again, and his chest was tight. No, they weren't kids any longer, but they were still playing games. "I let her get away. Again."

Suzie grasped his hand. "Jack, sit down. Go pull that lawn chair over here and sit for a minute. You and I are going to have a little talk."

Jack rolled his eyes. "Suzie, Sam will have my hide if I don't get this azalea in the ground before he gets back. Why don't you just talk to me while I'm working? I doubt anything you say is going to sink into my thick skull, anyway."

He turned back to his work.

"Giving up, aren't you?"

"Probably."

"You're still in love with her, though."

"Yep."

"And you're going to be a miserable SOB for the rest of your damn life because of it?"

Jack grinned and looked back at her. "I'm going to try like hell not to be."

"That's good."

"Why?"

"Because I'd hate for you to be miserable all night tonight at the lodge."

"The lodge?" Hell, that's right. There was that couples thing... "I'm not going."

Suzie stood. "Oh, yes, you are. I need a date. Brad's too busy in the kitchen, and I want to dance. I already have a sitter, so pick me up at seven. Got it?"

"Suzie...."

She glared at him. "Jack Ackerman, you're not going to mope around all day and night when you could be out having some fun and getting your mind off things."

"You're not going to try any of that matchmaking crap on me, are you?"

She chuckled. "I wouldn't dream of it. Just be here by seven."

———

JASMINE STOOD AT THE END OF A COUNTRY LANE, her car parked off to the side of the narrow, two-lane mountain road. A rusty mailbox sat planted on her left, and an even rustier cattle guard loomed before her.

She crossed the gate without incident and sauntered up the dirt road, wondering what she was going to say when she reached the house at the end, and if the person who lived there would open the door and let her in.

She just wanted to talk. That's all. And there was so much she wanted to say and to understand.

Breathing deep, she moved on. One foot in front of the other. Step by step up the old porch. Two strides to the door.

Knock. Knock. Knock.

The inside door swung open. She stared at him through the screen door. His face was full of questions. For a moment, neither of them said a word.

"Jasmine?"

She nodded. "Hi, Daddy. May I come in?"

———

WHY IN THE WORLD I LET HER TALK ME INTO THIS, I'll never know.

The last place Jack needed to be tonight was a couples

function. Everywhere he turned, there were pairs. Dancing. Eating together. Kissing.

What was Suzie thinking?

What was *he* thinking?

Jack wasn't certain.

The couples thing was a benefit for the local hospital. An annual event, and Suzie's husband, Brad, always offered the lodge for no charge. Brad and Suzie together catered the event and footed the bill, while the townspeople and local artisans offered their wares up for silent auction.

It was for a damned good cause, but he wasn't up for the whole shenanigans. So, he bid on a couple items and slipped Suzie a donation before they arrived.

He'd done his part.

Now, at fifteen minutes after eight, Jack was ready to move on.

If Jasmine had been here, though, he could have danced all night, and he was pretty darned sure he'd have had the most beautiful women in the room on his arm.

He scanned the crowd looking for Suzie and, not seeing her, decided she must be back in the kitchen with her husband. His brother, Sam, and sister-in-law, Becca, were talking to another couple across the room. Jack gave him the high sign and tipped his head toward the door, which was man-code for 'I'm outta here.' Sam nodded back with a thumbs up.

Can't wait to get back home.

But he couldn't leave without telling Suzie, even if it meant risking another talk. He headed off toward the kitchen.

Suzie met him as he rounded a corner, Brad at her side.

"Jack!"

"Hey Suzie. Brad. Listen, I'm going to head out."

Suzie smiled and hooked her arm with her husband's. "That's fine, Jack. I hope you had a good time. I know this is not a singles thing—it might have been more fun for you if it was—but it sure beats sitting alone in that big ol' house of yours."

Actually, that sounded pretty good to him right now, but he simply nodded and agreed. "It was real nice, Suzie. Thanks for asking me."

"Thanks for bringing me up. Brad will see me home."

Brad reached out to shake Jack's hand. "Thanks, man. Glad you could come."

Jack shook back. "Wouldn't have missed it. Keep doing the good work."

He lifted his hand to wave goodbye but stopped when Brad spoke again. "I hear you are doing some good work yourself."

"Excuse me?"

"For Ms. Leinie. The new family center over on Court Street."

Jack sighed. Had that gotten around town already? "There are still a lot of details to work out," he told him. "But the building is on schedule and will finish on time."

"That's great. I heard Ms. Leinie left Jasmine Walker the money to run the operation. That true?"

Suzie nudged Brad in the side and smirked. Jack almost laughed. "Man, secrets don't last long in Harbor Falls, do they?"

"It's Harbor Falls, Jack. There are no secrets," Suzie said.

He nodded. "But to answer your question, yes, Ms. Leinie left Jasmine the funds to operate the family center, but there were...um, stipulations, and Jasmine is, well...still thinking it over."

Suzie perked up. "Really?"

"No. Not really. I just made that up."

"But you wish she were just thinking it over?"

Jack agreed. "Yes. That's why I've asked the bank to give

her a few more days to see if she comes around. I don't know if she will, but—"

"But you can hope. Hot damn, there is still some spunk left in you. I was worried."

Suzie stepped forward and looked up into his face, determination spread all over hers. She might be petite, but her manner packed a punch. "Jack Ackerman, what the hell are you doing waiting around for that girl to make some sort of decision? Go the heck after her!"

Jack backed up. "Whoa. No, you got that wrong. She walked away from everything. I'm just hoping she'll reconsider."

"Then you're going to have to nudge her."

"I want to respect her wishes."

Suzie's hands went to her hips. "Well, you can respect her wishes until you are old and gray but that doesn't warm your bed at night! Man up, Jack. Go get her and bring her back here. Do it now."

"Now?"

"There's no time like the present."

A sense of urgency struck him. Jack turned and headed for the door.

The drive home took approximately fifteen minutes normally. But Jack took his time on the winding mountain roads, letting many people's words rattle around inside his brain. His. Suzie's. Jasmine's.

It was the first time all day he'd had a few quiet minutes to himself. To think. Hell, for the past few days he'd kept himself busy at the nursery and with clients, as well as at the construction site on Court Street.

Busy hands, busy mind. *There you go, push everything out except the task at hand.*

He'd had plenty to keep himself occupied. If he could, his brain would stop replaying Jasmine's last words:

*And I'm looking at you right now and telling you, with all of my heart, that I love you back. I **always** have, and I **always** will. But I'm not the woman to give you those babies. I'm not the woman to sleep in your bed. I can't. I can't give you babies. I can't live here. And I can't love you like you want me to love you.*

Those words played on an endless loop in his head for the past two days. *I can't, I can't, I can't.* Not that she wouldn't, but that she *can't.*

What the hell did that really mean? *Can't?*

He was going to find out.

He might have let Jasmine go once when he was too young to do anything about it, but he wasn't about to let her go a second time. Times have changed, and he was older. Dammit. No matter what, he wasn't stopping until he brought her home.

Jack glanced at his watch. Eight-thirty-five. Time enough to throw some clothes in a bag and drive like hell. He could be in Atlanta by midnight or so. He didn't know how he would find her, but he sure as hell knew people who could help him along the way. By the time he got to Atlanta, he expected to have an address.

He picked up his cell phone and dialed.

"Hello?"

"Suzie?"

"Jack? What's wrong?"

"Not a thing. Just taking your advice, but I need your help."

"You got it."

"Either start working some of your matchmaking magic shit or Google the hell out of Jasmine's name and get me an address. I'm heading to Atlanta."

Chapter Twelve

Jasmine set her bag by the door and followed the wraparound porch all the way to the back of the house. She stood for a moment, taking in the calming view of the moon shining down over Falls Lake, the mountains providing the perfect balance of backdrop.

Breathing deep, and exhaling a long cleansing breath, she moved closer to the railing and looked up into the sky.

There's you, Gemini. And there's me, Aquarius.

She studied the stars. They still looked the same, hadn't changed, of course. People change though. They get born, grow up, and die, all while the stars stay steady in the sky. Fixed in their twinkling spots.

How had fifteen years gone by in such a hurry? Jasmine could still remember how free it felt to lie in the back of Jack's pickup truck, staring up at that big sky, wrapped in a sleeping bag. How wonderful it was to lay enclosed up in his arms. And his love.

She marveled how Jack's love was unwavering. Fixed. Like the stars.

Her love for him was like that years ago, too. But now? It

seemed skittish, like a moving target. She'd spent the last few days dodging his shooting stars.

How could she have let fifteen years come between them?

She lowered her gaze, staring at the triangle of moon glow rippling on the lapping currents. That wasn't true. She had often thought of Jack. There were times she'd even considered driving up to Harbor Falls. But something always stopped her. The secrets stopped her.

Her pregnancy. The baby's death.

"Well, all of that is out in the open now," she whispered.

She glanced at her watch, wondering where Jack was. She'd hoped they could talk tonight. She had a lot to say. And she had a lot of listening to do, too, if only he would be open to it.

She wouldn't blame him if he wouldn't.

It was Saturday night; he could be anywhere, she supposed. Maybe getting a bite to eat. Perhaps visiting with his parents. Maybe he had a date.

"Shit."

She didn't think about that. Does he date? They hadn't really talked about things like that. They hadn't really gotten into anything personal at all.

How well did she really know Jack now?

How well did he know her?

Not well at all, truly. Then why was she standing here on his deck, ready to pour out her heart and soul to him, in one last attempt to right a fifteen-year-old wrong?

"Good luck with that," she whispered. Matters of the heart don't subscribe to wisdom. At least in her world.

Now she was second-guessing herself. Perhaps she'd been wrong to just show up. Hang out on his deck while he wasn't home. She should get a room somewhere. Maybe at that inn he told her about. She could leave a note and maybe they could meet for breakfast. Besides, it's really rude to just camp out on someone's deck like a....

"Shit. Like a stalker."

Jasmine turned and retraced her steps. Rounding the corner, she stopped up short. There he was, standing on the porch, staring at her bag by the door. "Jack?"

JACK, 1999

Jack paced in front of his truck, parked behind the old meeting house, nervous and a little scared. Jasmine was supposed to have been there at ten-thirty. The plan was for her to sneak away from the graduation party Ms. Leinie was throwing tonight with the other foster kids and then make her way downtown through the side streets to this parking area.

The time was now ten-fifty, and she wasn't there yet.

His stomach clutched with worry.

In his truck cab, he had everything they would need for a while. He'd packed a suitcase of clothing. There was a cooler full of food in the back—enough to get them by for a couple of days until they found an apartment in Asheville and could go grocery shopping. He'd borrowed a few things from his parents' house—some towels and washcloths, sheets and pillowcases. He had enough money in his pocket for a couple nights' hotel costs, and the deposit and first month's rent of an apartment. He'd been watching the papers and knew how much it was going to cost them. They'd be good for a month or so and he'd be looking for work as soon as they were settled.

It was all planned out. Everything was in place.

Except for Jasmine.

The clock on the side of the bank building chimed. Eleven o'clock. Thirty minutes late. Had something happened to her? Could she not get out of the house? Did she forget?

No, she wouldn't have forgotten. She had anticipated this night as much as he had.

Something was wrong.

Jack pulled himself up into the truck cab and sat. Waiting. Watching. He stayed awake as long as he could. Finally, his eyelids grew heavy.

JASMINE, 1999

I pulled my backpack from underneath the bleachers in the baseball dugout, dusted it off with my hand and slung it over my shoulder. I'd ditched the party at Ms. Leinie's without a hitch, which was probably going to be the easiest thing I would do all evening.

Not that leaving Ms. Leinie was easy. It wasn't.

Edging the shadows of the security lights, I walked the perimeter of the school and then crossed the road. Moving quickly for several blocks, I was glad the traffic was light, but also a little worried about being out so late. I'm not accustomed to being out on the streets by myself at this time of night.

I glanced at my watch. Ten-fifty-five. How long would Jack wait?

My gut ached, but I pushed that sensation aside. Not now. There were things to get through here, and I didn't have time for regret or worry. No time to contemplate what I should, or should not, have done. I just had to keep putting one foot in front of the other and move forward.

The bus station was around the corner. My aunt's address and phone number were in my pocket. In my backpack were some clothes that soon wouldn't fit, my diploma rolled up into a little tube, and a stash of cash I'd earned babysitting this past year.

It was a start.

What I didn't have was a sense of the future. All I knew was that a baby was on the way, and that Jack was no longer in my life.

I got to the station, bought a ticket, and visited the restroom before boarding. When it was time, I stepped onto the bus, stowed my bag at my feet, and silently said goodbye to Harbor Falls. At midnight, the bus rolled down Main Street, on the way out of town toward the interstate. We passed the old meeting house, and I saw the taillights of Jack's truck reflect the bus headlights as we passed.

A painful, panicky thud hit my gut.

He was still sitting there. Waiting.

I watched for as long as I could until the bus rounded a corner.

Then I curled into my seat and cried all the way to Atlanta.

AT FIRST JACK THOUGHT HIS EYES WERE PLAYING tricks on him. He'd noticed her car as he drove up his driveway, and her bag sitting by the door as he ascended the porch steps. So preoccupied the past few minutes, thinking about what he was going to do when he found her in Atlanta, the reality that she *was here now*—at his home—was a little unsettling.

As he reached for the bag, Jasmine stepped around the corner.

He straightened. "Jasmine? What are you doing here?"

"I..." She stepped closer. "Jack, I was waiting for you, but..." She was actually wringing her hands, shifting from one foot to another. Antsy. Glancing off and back to him again. Nervous?

"But what?"

"But I decided to leave. I shouldn't have come here without calling you first. I didn't mean to impose." She edged toward the steps. "Maybe we can get together tomorrow and talk about... About some of the stuff that happened this week."

"Stuff?"

"You know, with Ms. Leinie's estate. And well, with us."

Jack narrowed his gaze. "So 'us' is running a close second behind the estate issue?"

She shook her head. "I didn't mean it like that, Jack. Look, I'm trying here, but maybe I came at a bad time. I can come back tomorrow."

"No." *Over my dead body.* Jack set her bag back down on the porch floor and walked determinedly toward her. "You are not going anywhere, Jasmine. C'mere."

Her eyes widened as he grasped her upper arms and hauled her up against him. Before she could protest, Jack captured her lips with his, warming them with his touch. Her skin was chilly, which told him she had probably stood out there for a while, and all he could think about was how he wanted to warm every inch of her skin later—if she would let him.

Jasmine whimpered beneath his mouth. He deepened the kiss, and her arms circled his neck. He knew they had a way to go, but damn, this was a good start.

Pulling back, he peered into her eyes. "So, I'll ask again." His voice softened. "What are you doing here, Jasmine?"

"I want to talk."

"Just so you know," he warned, "I want more than talk."

One corner of her mouth shot up in a half-grin. "So do I," she admitted. "We can get there, but there are some things I need to say first."

"The last time I let you talk didn't go too well for me."

She huffed out a breath and closed her eyes. "I know. I'm sorry, Jack. That was so wrong. I hope you can forgive me."

That warmed his heart immensely. "Jasmine, I damned near drove to Atlanta tonight to see you. I just stopped off here to grab a few things."

"So, you were expecting to stay awhile in Atlanta?"

"You said you couldn't live here. Maybe I could live there."

Jasmine blinked. "You don't mean that."

"If it means having you in my life, then yes. I would do that."

"Oh, Jack." Jasmine sighed. "I would never ask you to give up your life in Harbor Falls."

He held her gaze steadily. "You weren't asking."

"But you were coming anyway?"

"I was hoping to talk some sense into you, Jazzy. Maybe come to a compromise, somehow. But now that you are...."

"Now, I'm here."

He nodded. "Yes. You're here. For how long, Jasmine?"

"For as long as it takes."

He grinned wide. "That might take a while." He leaned in and gave her another quick kiss on the lips. "But I'm willing to work on it."

Jasmine sighed and smiled. "I'm the one who has more work to do, I think, but I figure if we're going to be working together, we'll get everything ironed out."

"Working together?"

"Yeah. At the family center."

Jack's heart jolted. She really meant it. "You're sure?"

"Yes. It's time for me to leave Atlanta, Jack. It's time for me to come home and pay attention to the kids in my own backyard."

Jack's heart swelled. He wasn't sure his chest was going to hold it in. "I'll call the bank on Monday to tell them you've changed your mind."

She placed her hands on his chest and snuggled closer to him. "I called Art this afternoon. It's all taken care of. Just a few details on Monday."

"Have you thought of everything?"

"No. Definitely not. There are some things that are just going to take care of themselves. In time."

"Such as?"

"Such as letting the past go and not repeating history. Such as leaving you behind and not telling you about the baby. I should have told you, and I want to apologize for that. All I can say is I was young and scared and stupid."

"Not stupid. Young and scared is enough. And Jasmine, it's something we need to work through, but you're right—we need to let the past go and we need to look forward."

Smiling, she nodded. "I love you, Jack. For everything. But it all still scares me somewhat. Coming back to Harbor Falls, living here, being with you, maybe having children one day..."

"Jasmine, honey, you won't be alone."

She nodded against his chest. "I know." She paused and then added. "And that is the most comforting part. I don't want to be alone anymore, Jack. I want to be with you."

His heart swelled, and he hauled her up against him. "God, Jazzy, that's all I want, for us to be together." He held her tight, and they both released long-held breaths. Jack physically felt her shoulders relax.

"I saw my father today," she whispered after a moment.

Jack eased back and looked at her. "Really? Where is he?"

"Not far, actually. A little place in the mountains about ten miles out of town. I learned some things about my mother and their marriage. I also know why he went to prison, and why he never tried to find me when he got out."

"Why was that?"

"He thought I was better off without him."

"What do you think?"

"I think I need him now more than I realized. And he needs me." Jasmine's eyes searched his face. "But most of all, I need you more than ever," she whispered. She shifted her stance and drew her sweater tighter across her chest. "Jack, if we are together, I have to make certain that no one in this town is going to treat you differently because you are with me. And if we have children, it will kill me to think they would go through the kinds of things I went through in school. I know times have changed and a lot of years have passed, but children can be cruel and sometimes adults can be too. I don't want our children to suffer through that."

Jack cupped her face in his hands. "Jasmine... My sweet, sweet Jasmine," he said. "Don't you realize? Because of who you are, and who I am, our children will be fine. I know it was difficult for you, but your parents didn't pave an easy path. Our children will have us, and we will make that path as smooth as we possibly can."

"But we can't control everything."

"No, we can't. But we can prepare them for times when we aren't beside them."

Jasmine closed her eyes. "You, Jack Ackerman, are going to make an excellent father. But I always knew that."

"And you are going to make beautiful babies."

"We will make beautiful babies." She hesitated and then added, "I want our children to know my father, their grandfather. He is not a bad person, just made some bad choices. And he deserves a chance."

"We all deserve a second chance, Jasmine."

Smiling, she agreed. "Yes, we do."

Jack nodded. "Are you still scared?"

"Out of my wits. You?"

"Not me," he answered. "I'm in love."

Her grin spread across her face. "I'm in love, too, and

that's why I am so scared. I never want to be separated from you again."

"No worries," he told her. Jack played with her hair and kissed her forehead, holding her as close as possible to his heart. "I'd cross the sky for you, Jazzy."

Epilogue

Six months later...

Mendelssohn's *Wedding March* drifted through the park across the street from the old meeting house. A small crowd gathered on the lawn for a rather unconventional joining of a hometown couple.

Jack Ackerman, wearing his fifteen-year-old Harbor Falls football jersey, leaned against his 1998 Chevy Silverado pickup truck, waiting for his bride to join him.

Jasmine Walker, wearing her white graduation dress and carrying a bright orange backpack, slowly made her way toward him. Smiling.

They paused beside the truck, gazes locked, while the bride's father stepped forward to hand his daughter over to his new son-in-law. Those close by could hear him respond with, "Her mother and I," when Reverend Peters asked who gave the bride.

While the crowd listened, the minister asked the couple to repeat their vows. They didn't mince words, and then Jack Ackerman took his bride's face into his hands and kissed her thoroughly, while the onlookers in the park cheered.

Quickly, as if making a get-away, the newlywed couple scrambled into the cab of the four-wheel-drive truck and made their escape to their honeymoon destination—a night wrapped up in a sleeping bag, lying in the back of their pickup truck, watching the stars and listening to the waves of Falls Lake lap the shore.

So maybe sometimes you can go home again.

A Note from Maddie

Dear Reader Friends,

Star Crossed is one of my favorite books. I recently reread the story, and I still cry every time. Growing up in a small town myself, I can feel Jasmine's pain, and Jack's heartache. I hope you enjoyed their story and felt their emotions, too. Thanks for reading.

One of the best ways to tell others if you liked the book (or not!) is to leave a review at Goodreads, or at the bookstore where you purchased it. You can also leave reviews at my website, maddiejamesbooks.com.

Ready for more Sweet Hart Inn? Scroll on to read the first chapter of *Not This Christmas,* where Nora Patterson and the Reverend Rock Peters find themselves temporarily snowbound in a mountain cabin. What could happen there, you ask?

Not This Christmas

Not This
Christmas – Chapter One

"I really hate to say this," Suzie Hart announced, drawing back a drapery panel and peering out her living room window. "Because I'm having so much fun and I don't want anyone to leave, but if you have to drive anywhere other than Harbor Falls, you might think about leaving soon."

The crowd in Suzie's living room twittered and chattered about.

"Ah, Suzie. It's just a little snow squall," Jack Ackerman explained. "It will be here and gone. Nothing to worry about."

His wife, Jasmine, stepped closer to the window and stood beside Suzie. "I don't know, Jack. Take a look." The two women stared out the window. "Living in Atlanta for so long, I'd forgotten what snow can be like in the mountains," she added. "Should we leave?"

Jack shrugged. "We have four-wheel drive. We'll be fine."

"Is it getting bad out there, girls?" Sydney Hart stepped into the group. "I've been having so much fun I hadn't paid attention to the weather."

Nora Patterson hadn't either. She glanced over at the crowd in Suzie's living room. Some of them appeared to be a tad anxious. "I'm heading to Dad's farm, near Dalton Springs. Maybe I should think about heading out."

Jack turned and met her gaze. "You have to drive over there tonight?"

"It's Christmas Eve. I don't want Dad to be alone."

He nodded. "Right."

Paying more attention to the weather might have been a good idea, Nora.

But she'd not missed a Holiday Open House at Sweet Hart Inn since Suzie and her husband Brad hosted it the first year they were married—and she really didn't want to miss this one.

There would be a silent auction later that evening, with the proceeds going to Miss Leinie's Place, a local family shelter. The community hosted many events to support the shelter, and Suzie's holiday open house was one of them. The shelter provided services for children and families—mostly for foster kids and those at risk, but also for families and anyone in need. Earlier today, Nora had dropped off a half-dozen boxes of gently used children's books for Christmas presents. She had also donated a new set of Christmas picture books for Suzie's silent auction.

Nora loved Harbor Falls and wanted nothing more than to be an integral part of the community—personally and business-wise.

She'd moved into town from the farm after graduating from college with a degree in library science and then taking over the family bookstore. She'd grown up out in the county, on the other side of Dalton Springs, and although she loved country life, found that she also liked the convenience of small-town living—especially after experiencing bigger city college life in central Ohio.

Columbus, in fact. The Ohio State University.

Which was actually an incredibly rewarding experience,

and one she was glad she'd had—*Go Bucks!* But now, she was extremely happy and content living in her small-town mountain world.

It was also fun since she and Suzie are good friends now. And, because her best friend, Becca—who had also grown up, and still lived, in Harbor Falls—had finally stopped talking about moving away now that she'd married Sam Ackerman.

Of course, Harbor Falls was where Sam's brother, Nora's ex-boyfriend, Jack Ackerman, also lived. Keyword 'ex' boyfriend. The 'ex' boyfriend, who had recently married his high school sweetheart, Jasmine—an Atlanta attorney who moved back to Harbor Falls unexpectedly and now managed Miss Leinie's Place. All that happened a few months ago, not long, actually, after Jack and Nora broke up.

But she was over that now.

Mostly.

She glanced over at the happy couple and smiled. Jasmine grinned and waved back.

Nora knew they were happy. She could tell, and actually, she was thrilled for them.

It wasn't so much that she missed Jack. She missed being part of a couple. One day, perhaps she'd find her own true love. She'd even hired Suzie Hart once as a matchmaker!

But that didn't pan out, of course.

Maybe Santa would grant her wish this year. She'd been a good girl. Pretty much. She'd even prayed on it, but it seemed God hadn't thought it was time for her.

Yet.

She remained hopeful.

But not this Christmas. True love for her this Christmas would likely not happen. Especially since Christmas was simply hours away.

An hour later, Nora gripped the steering wheel of her shiny new red Camaro and leaned forward, as if pushing her face closer to the windshield would actually help her see better. The visibility was awful. In fact, worse than awful. The weatherman on the radio called it near whiteout conditions.

She had no business being out in this mess—in her shiny new red Camaro or in any vehicle. She should have headed out hours ago, quietly excusing herself and citing the weather. She *should* have called her father and told him she was on her way and would be at his home in Dalton Springs in time for Christmas Eve dinner—but she didn't.

And she should have double-checked her purse for her cell phone before leaving the inn.

Of course, she knew right where it was, sitting on Suzie Hart Matthews' side table in the living room. How could she forget it?

But she didn't do any of those things.

A host of other *should-haves* ran through her head.

Should have checked the weather.

Should have worn boots rather than heels.

Should have stayed home in Harbor Falls.

But no. She had to be the social butterfly and flit from one holiday scene to another, because that's what Nora Patterson does. Flit. Be social. Still, she should have taken precautions. Besides, her father was expecting her, and she didn't want to disappoint him. The days were lonely for him since her mother had passed earlier in the year.

"Please, God, just get me get to Dad's. I can't walk in snow in these shoes if I get stranded." Besides, her legs were freezing.

Should have worn pants.

If it hadn't been that she was having such a great time at Suzie's annual Christmas Eve open house, she wouldn't have lost track of time.

"Come on, Santa, and God, and anyone else out there

who is listening—" she leaned forward again and peered up into the darkening sky, "Time to work some Christmas magic. If you plan to bring me a future husband for Christmas this year, times a-wastin'. It's Christmas Eve already..."

She sighed. From her lips to God's ears, but she had her doubts.

"But I'd really be happy if you just got me safely to the farm."

Shaking her head, she concentrated on her driving and wished she were back at Suzie's.

As usual, her friend's home was warm and welcoming. A fire lit up the hearth in the living room. Cinnamon sticks and dried orange peel added a holiday zip to the house coffee blend, which not only smelled but tasted heavenly on this blustery day. She wished she had a cup of that yummy coffee right now—not to mention cookies. She had sampled more than her share of Suzie's Christmas confections. Plus, the Jam Cake with gooey caramel glaze was nearly sinful—the thick slice she'd devoured later in the afternoon had made her happy and cozy.

She'd just have to keep that warm memory in her head until she got to her dad's place.

Nora licked her lips just thinking about it. She'd definitely stayed too long. Suzie had even wanted her to spend the night.

Should have spent the night.

With the back of her gloved hand, she attempted to wipe away condensation building up on the inside of her windshield and wondered if her defroster wasn't working properly. Squinting, she cranked up the heat and peered out the hole. Her headlamps made two funnels of light pushing out in front of the car, with a snow-sleet mixture slanting into the beam.

A knot curled in her stomach. She had about a thirty-minute drive to her father's home—on a good day, and this wasn't a good day. Even though she didn't have to go over Falls Mountain, she had to go through the foothills and around the lake. The road was narrow and curvy in places. The evening was only going to get darker and the snow deeper. Never in her life had she seen the white stuff come down so hard and so fast. With dusk falling and the snow, the visibility was getting worse. The ruts in the road looked at least a couple of inches deep already.

Ruts. Someone had come this way before her, not very long ago. Some other fool, she guessed. Then, just as she had that thought, she saw the brake lights flash in front of her, like someone was intentionally pushing a foot on and off the brake, warning her to—

Stop?!

She slammed on her own brakes, gripped the steering wheel tighter, and braced herself.

"Not. Gonna!"

The Camaro fishtailed, and its back end slid to the right, swinging around and clipping the tail end of the vehicle in the road. She spun again and shrieked, losing all sense of direction, the car moving of its own accord. By then she had released the steering wheel and covered her face with her hands.

Sweet Jesus, take the wheel!

With a crunch of metal against something super solid, the vehicle came to an abrupt, jolting halt. Nora's body thrust to the left, and her head cracked against the driver's side window. Pain shot through her temple, and then just as quickly as it had all started, her world went black.

Reverend Rockford Peters nearly cursed when his old Chevy Blazer stalled on Lake Road at the foot of Falls Mountain. *Nearly cursed* being the operative words. He wasn't averse to slewing an occasional *expletive deleted* when the timing was right, and he was alone, and the situation warranted it—but he tried like heck to rein in those expletives when he could because he didn't want to let one slip in front of his parishioners. He had a reputation to uphold, after all.

He stared at the flat-lined bars on his cell phone, and his stomach sank. He knew the general vicinity of where he was, but the storm had disoriented him a little. He'd been heading back home after attending an afternoon service near Asheville to put the finishing touches on his own candlelight service at the Methodist Church in Harbor Falls, when his bald tires had skidded on the slick mush.

Should have bought new tires before winter. But he'd spent that money on Christmas gifts for the foster kids' party at Miss Leinie's place. Jasmine Walker Ackerman had been more than appreciative, and the smiles on the kids' faces had warmed his heart.

That was worth it—even if he was going to be temporarily inconvenienced right now.

Next paycheck, new tires. He mentally put that on his to-do list. In the meantime, he would keep those warm smiles on his mind as he figured out how to get through the next few hours and get home.

The cold front had raced over the mountain unexpectedly, leaving in its wake a mess of freezing rain, followed by sleet and a pelting snowstorm. And right about now, with his right tire off the edge of the road, and the back end of his vehicle sticking out cockeyed over the two-lane, he wanted to spit out the most satisfying expletive he could muster. Preferably one that started and ended with a hard consonant sound.

Lights in his rearview mirror caught his eye.

He pumped his brakes. "Dammit!"

The car behind him slid sideways, from what he gathered as he watched its headlights arc off the mountain wall. The vehicle's passenger side slammed into his rear end and pushed the Blazer further onto the shoulder. The Chevy rocked a bit, and he held his breath, not ready to ride this thing down the small slope he feared was there. He watched the lights behind him spin again and twist back the other way, heard another screeching crash, and then silence.

He sat there for a moment, unsure of his next move. The only sounds were the ice pellets hitting his windshield and an increasing creaking noise coming from somewhere underneath his vehicle.

Too quiet. What about the people in the other car? He heard nothing, and that concerned him.

Fishing a flashlight out from under his seat, he pushed open the driver's side door and stepped out into the weather. An icy blast cut into his face as he stood, narrowed his gaze, and glanced behind his truck. The other car's lights were still on; the beams aimed toward the trees to his left. The snow was coming down thick and heavy now, already building up on the roof of the red sports car. He stepped toward the vehicle and flashed his light, the beam landing on the driver's side window. His stomach clutched when he saw the smear of blood on the glass and a mass of long blond hair.

"Damn. I mean, oh good Lord. Please help her." *Maybe this is why I'm here.*

He rushed as best he could through the slush toward the woman and lifted the door latch. The door opened, and she fell like dead weight toward the ground. With a combination of what he supposed was pure adrenaline and sheer determination, he caught her up and lifted her into his arms. Her head fell back, slack. Her eyes closed. Her red lipstick-stained lips slightly parted.

Rock looked into her face, heaved in a deep breath, and shifted her body to where her face was nestled snug against his chest, and out of the driving wind. He didn't recognize the woman. She definitely was not one of his parishioners. He also knew she needed help. *His* help. And he had to see that she got it.

He straightened and stared at his surroundings. Snow. Trees. The mountain and rocks behind him he knew, because he could barely see past the wet snow curtaining his view. Briefly, he closed his eyes. "Please, God, show me the way. Oh, and sorry about those two expletives."

He opened his eyes again. The snow slowly let up. As best he could, he played the flashlight over the scene and scanned the horizon. Trees. More trees. And there. A mailbox. Or the remnants of one, at least. The post was bent, and the box itself was on the ground, but at least it was evidence of a residence at some time, past or present.

Right?

Beside of the post, there appeared to be a break in the tree line.

A lane? A gravel drive leading somewhere?

"I'll take that," he whispered. "Thank you." As if warning him not to linger, a gust of snow blew up into his face, cold and wet, and temporarily blinding him. "I'm moving, Lord. Just let me get her safe and warm."

Carefully, he slipped the flashlight into his pocket, the beam shining up into the night. Enough to light his way. For now. He started toward the mailbox, snow slanting into his face. Once he got into the clearing and headed back through the trees, the snow dissipated somewhat, but the wind cut right through him. The woman grew heavier in his arms, but he refused to think about that, and kept putting one foot straight in front of the other.

Step after step, after step.

One leap of faith at a time.

When he thought he could go no further, when his knees were about to buckle and he could no longer feel his hands, he shuffled a few steps more and hit something solid with the toe of his boot.

He blinked and stared down through watery, stinging eyes. A porch step.

He glanced up. A cabin.

Thank you.

Nora groaned. Her body shifted and then rolled onto something lumpy. A dull throbbing pain radiated through her forehead and around to the back of her head. She tried to blink but found that one simple action difficult, and with each effort to flutter her eyelids open, she failed.

Cold. So cold.

She had a vague remembrance of someone. Of being held and maybe carried. Of wind, sharp and biting. Of an occasional deep voice saying things like, "I'll take care of you," and "We'll get you warm soon. Promise." Of her hands and legs shaking and then going numb.

Then nothing else until now.

She curled onto her side seeking warmth and found some by burrowing deeper into something scratchy. Didn't matter. Her face was warmer now. Her legs and hands tingled, and that made all the difference in the world. Tingling meant she was alive. Right?

Her brain fuzzy, she felt disoriented, but the warmth cloaked her inside a happy place for a moment—then she faded back into a black void.

Learn more about *Not This Christmas* on my website, or purchase at your favorite bookstore.

More Harbor Falls Books!

Cozy up at the inn where the heart of the Blue Ridge beats strongest...

Welcome to Sweet Hart Inn, a charming bed and breakfast nestled along the peaceful shores of Falls Lake, at the foot of Falls Mountain. At the center of it all is chef and innkeeper Suzie Hart, whose kitchen is always warm, and whose heart is always open. Together with her husband Brad, Suzie serves up matchmaking advice and comfort food, along with second chances, and a generous helping of happily ever after.

The Sweet Hart Inn Books

All of My Heart
Take My Heart
Match My Heart
Tame My Heart
The Dating Game
Miss Matched Hearts
The Husband List
Chase My Heart
No Sweeter Match
One More Kiss

The Falls Mountain Books

Welcome to Falls Mountain, and the quaint town of Harbor Falls.

Tucked deep into the Blue Ridge Mountains, bricked streets, lakeside views, and charming local shops set the scene for small town romance.

In this standalone-but-interconnected series, you'll meet bakers, bookstore owners, chocolatiers, school teachers, and more—all trying to run their businesses, chase their dreams, and keep their hearts in check. But in Harbor Falls, love has a habit of showing up unannounced...

From second chances to secret babies to grumpy-sunshine pairings, each book brings a satisfying happily-ever-after and a cast of characters you'll want to visit again and again.

Falls Mountain Romance is a companion series to the Sweet Hart Inn Romance books by Maddie James.

Dance into My Heart
The Christmas Nanny
The Heartbreaker
Star Crossed

Not This Christmas
Convince My Heart

I hope you'll check out these books, and my other series, on
my website at:
www.maddiejamesbooks.com

About Maddie James

Romance with a pulse—small towns, big love, and a dash of drama.

Maddie James writes small-town romance with heart, heat, and the occasional haunting. Her stories range from sweet to spicy, suspenseful to supernatural—happily-ever-afters guaranteed! From stand-alone love stories to binge-worthy series, Maddie delivers love next door, some cowboy kisses, an occasional hint of danger, and just enough drama to keep things interesting.

Get all the drama delivered to your inbox when you sign-on to Maddie's VIP reader list!

Free books, sneak peaks, bonus content, giveaways, and more...

Learn more: maddiejamesbooks.com/pages/newsletter

www.ingramcontent.com/pod-product-compliance
Lightning Source LLC
Chambersburg PA
CBHW060231180626
46813CB00007B/3039